PRESENTS

N.O.M.A.

L.K.BROOKS-SIMPSON

Titles available in the IXI PRESS series (in reading order):

First Published in Great Britain in 2024

N.O.M.A.

ISBN Print edition 978-1-912791-05-7

This book is dedicated to all who have been victim of war crimes and unjust political movements.

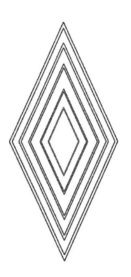

CHAPTER 1

Guerillas in Guyana

NORU LOGS – (2012) Present Day

Unknown user: Hello, hello? How does this thing work?

NORU: Node-Operations-Management-System online. Running facial recognition scans. Noru speaking

Unknown user: Stop doing that-

NORU: Facial scan completed. Storing in personnel database.

Unknown user: You see this case you are in? It stops any feedback signals to the main suit.

NORU: Unknown user, please return me to Bunker 55. I have been given instructions to monitor the Spectre.

Unknown user: The Spectre is not going anywhere. He has been sitting in there for months. I just want to know one thing.

NORU: What is that one thing?

Unknown user: What exactly is N.O.M.A. supposed to be?

NORU: N.O.M.A. is the sole vigilante of Indiana's city, Heavens Conquest. He was first known for his acts against city crime but has become popularized, by public standard, for his forceful resignation of many of Indiana's corrupt politicians. The most notable of these politicians are: Sheena Habib, Milo Davies and Reginald Harrison. N.O.M.A. is also known for his stand against Boston Armies violent treatment of protesters - written by Young & Oliver Trent Times in Manhattan, New York.

Unknown user: I meant what does N.O.M.A. stand for?

NORU: I believe that is two questions.

Unknown user: Can you just tell me, please?

NORU: N.O.M.A. is an acronym. Acronyms can take on different meanings, for example - N.O.M.A. refers to the title of my program: Node-Operation-Management-Systems. If you wish to know the meaning intended perhaps the best course would be to ask the person under the suit?

END OF TRANSMISSION

SHARPA RAINFOREST

GUYANA, SOUTH AMERICA

SKKTITITIT! – A petal to the blade.

The drilling gunfire of the Boeing Apache-Attack Helicopter cut through the humble rainforest of Guyana and in its path, leaves, legumes and lives were ripped apart. The aerial assault was only a fragment of a scene so mercilessness, that blood painted the green. Danger came at such a furious pace that soldiers had little, if any, time to grieve for lost partners. It was a place where agony turned into heartlessness faster than the Guerillas would charge from the ambush locations in their native garden. Quicker than how the hardened infantry of Boston's army would fire back in alarm. The Guerillas of Guyana versus the will of America. A battle that had been told before, but the assurance of war was that there was always a secret that incited the violence.

SKKTITITIT! – Again it rained.

Infantry with infant ambitions. Too small a scope than to look into nothing but their own, but baring a chest big enough to hold the scars of war. Intelligent enough to conduct attrition warfare strategies, but also too blindsided to battle the brainwash of cultural propaganda, moreover, the temptation of a soldiers salary. The differences between a man and a killer. Little difference between the tropical battleground and a cold winter.

SKKTITITIT! – Both a sinner and a saint.

In the eyes of both oppositions, only the other was to blame. Even then, the thin strings of politics were hard to be seen in the majestic, Sharpa Rainforest evergreen - let alone the fingertips of controlling dictatorships. Wars always lasted longer than the conversations to prevent them. The rebuttal was always subtle. Like a piece in a puzzle; what started a war was always overlooked by what could be gained by it, and during the assault on the Sharpa Rainforest on August 2012, no one's eyes were more alight than Kai Boston's.

"Lower into the forest. I know where the camp is," said Kai, to the operator of the scout helicopter.

"You know where the camp is, how?" one of the six members inside of the helicopter rose and like everybody else on board, he had 'United States - Intelligence personnel' emblazoned across an I.D. badge on his chest. Kai acknowledged the question with a raise of one of his slit eyebrows and nothing more. Afterward, another member of the Intel team took stand.

"He's right. You coordinated this whole attack, how did you even know that they were hiding this kind of tech in the first place? When we get our hands on this, we are gonna be top dogs! Even the government are gonna start hiring us again."

"Sounds promotion worthy," Kai noted, despite full knowledge that his father, who happened to be the leader of Boston's Base army, would not even bat an eyelid at his latest feat.

"Promotion worthy alright, kid. With a lead like this I wouldn't be surprised if you were even working for the enemy," laughter of agreement filled the inside of the helicopter, of which Kai mimicked coolly. His ability to blend in did not merely stop with the identical, camouflage jackets that their army were assigned. The volume of laughter fell along with the height of their air vehicle when it started its slow descent. The crew held on to passenger bars, the sides of the helicopter or each other to steady themselves. The youngest member, however, reached for an item in the utility storage located to the rear of the helicopter. When Kai began strapping parachute gear to himself, more questions took flight.

"What on earth are you doing?"

"A parachute is safety gear man, put that away."

"This is what happens when you put youngsters on a mission."

"He aint' really gonna jump."

"By the time we reach ground, it might too late for what I came for," Kai sized up the prospect of a twenty thousand foot fall.

"What did you come for?" came one of the crew.

"Information. Do you think I would come all the way out here and get nothing? I could have coordinated this in my bed back at Heavens Conquest," he said, squaring himself at the doorway now.

"You'll die before you reach the floor. Our soldiers haven't even cleared all of the Guerillas from the forest yet."

"Whatever you say," Kai replied. The first and sternest member of the crew pulled himself toward the young recruit until they faced on.

When he looked at Kai directly, he saw oriental facial features on a Caucasian base. Korean pinewood coloured iris' hid behind angular eyes and an angular slit in each of his eyebrows made his appearance one of a kind. His long, wavy fringe sat kindly atop his head, emphasized by his tapered sides. His forehead was small, his bone structure was taught and this taught law governed the rest of his gracile, five foot ten build. The young man was undoubtedly lean, but undeniably conditioned and what his crew thought he lacked in maturity, he packed with surety.

"Who do you think you are, Boston?" he breathed into the side of Kai's face.

"Something you will never be, old man," Kai Boston fell forward to his peril, all the while his crew member was taken aback by his words. Kai Boston had a kamikaze for an ego; he would die before letting another best him.

In a sky filled with the blazing rays of the southern hemisphere and the blazing sounds of attack helicopter fire, the daring figure of Kai Boston sailed toward hostile ground. He could see the green vista reach for miles on end. It was a green was so fleshy, light could not breach. When his soaring frame finally broke through the natural awning, the calming of the war was before him. Silence. Emptiness. Instead of the pattering footsteps of battle, there was the slow crunch of twigs, dried leaves and collections of soil. Crickets, insects and birds now assumed their regular rainforest rhythms; a sibilance of clicks, tweets and twitters. Kai licked his teeth, as if in reprieve, it was now a bittersweet entrance to say the least.

BANG!

Just as he was to meet the ground, a gunshot fired. A bullet whispered when passing his right ear, before finding a target in his parachute. The only thing keeping him airborne. The sudden loss of resistance gave gravity a greater say and so, he took a painful tumble into the thick trunk of a nearby tree. Bark and centipedes landed centimeters from his face when he found himself floored.

"I remember ordering supply crates not a wannabe," came a voice filled with bass. When a round of prompt laughter followed, he knew exactly who it was.

"B*stard," Kai spat, upon looking up at, perhaps, his most hated person. He found his nose at the end of a pair of tabbing boots that belonged to his father, Sergeant Boston. The Sergeant had a squared face and like a square, there was no aspect of him that did not equal to the profile that most of America had drawn for him. Loud, literal and living on the edge of lividity.

"No one to use your kung fu moves on down here, boy. We took out those funky smelling guerillas already. Not a bad resting place either," between his derogatory remark was mild appreciation. The sheer magnitude of wildlife around them was a glorious example of nature, something their industrial community back in Indiana, U.S.A, could not recreate.

"One day it is going to be your life at risk and no one is going to save you,"

"Should have shot you too. The devil would probably get more work out of you down there," the Sergeant's comical routine began as his infantry began gathering amongst them.

"If I even left for a week the armies debts would be higher up your ass than these idiots. You know what we came for, now let's go before I change my mind," Kai took the parachute vest from his torso, alongside the laughter of all in attendance. Even though Boston's army boasted a battalion, a battle against his son was fruitless. Kai Boston's technical expertise could not be denied. Kai watched on gloatingly as his father grew increasingly pink in the face.

"It's hot in this damn country. Let's get to the damn village. Hopefully the thing this runt is leading us to is air conditioning," Sergeant Boston announced to his squadron of loyal followers, Kai however, was not fooled. He had exposed enough politicians to pick out a lie and he had experienced deference his entire life – he knew his father was immoral enough to use either tactic.

"Follow me," Kai said.

Boston's Army's exotic expedition began. The afternoon light beamed onto the travelers in the parts of the rainforest where the attack helicopter had decimated the canopy above. Kai observed the incisions in the green ceiling; in a way, it was almost as scarred as him. The only difference was nature always recovered, he could not. His past was as bleak as they came. He grew up as one of the few survivors in the genocide of his village in Korea and he was raised with the reality of being a product of rape. Both atrocities were committed by the country he now called home. Both atrocities indulged in by his father, for two products of lust; pay and pleasure. Having grown up with little to no memories of his family or country, for many years Kai tried to pay it no mind at the cost of the symptoms of denial. The regression; regret, withdrawal and trying to find his true meaning in life. If a rose could bloom in the blizzard – that was him; a cold demeanor and precepts of life and death that were so called, 'ice thin'. His culture was clawed from him at a young age; it was why he dedicated a large portion of his youth years to mastering the martial arts he had started back in his nameless village. So, to even have an ego was a privilege. Many thought his arrogance was a trait of the

Boston bloodline, but there was always hypocrisy in the ways of a sinner and a saint. Everything that he did was for the honour of Korea and not for his current Honaker. He was never understated about his strengths because there was no one else to carry his true family name. Before he knew it, they reached a dell in the Sharpa Rainforest which led to a small village by the forest stream.

"Here," Kai told those behind him.

"Where's this thing then? Looks like a normal sh!thole village to me," Sergeant Boston began at a yell,

"There," one of the infantry pointed to the near distance,

"Where?" the Sergeant retorted doggedly,

"There Sarge, kind of blending in with that tree,"

The Sergeant's eyes became that more bloodshot as he strained to see said device. When he finally caught sight of it, a wedge formed where his mouth was, revealing square, cut teeth.

"Get the attack helicopters to my location. If any of these f@$kers even step a toe out of these huts, I want you to light the whole place up," he chuckled into his radio. The Sergeant bumped shoulders with his son before continuing his wide legged stride toward the village. His assembly stepped when he did; consisting, it seemed, of practiced soldiers and volunteer studio crowds. When the last soldier had stepped, Kai followed closely behind. Eventually the foot soldiers reached the device that had indeed been painted with an earthly tone, to blend in with the surroundings at eye level.

"I just checked the huts, there is no one inside."

"They must have made a run for it, but they left us a little gift behind. These guerillas are nifty alright. But all good things must end. Someone put this thing offline," at their leader's request, a soldier fired several rounds into the barrel shaped device.

"Sir," one of the intel officers looked at his tracker in awe, "all of the signals on this part of the island just came on. And there are a lot coming from that hut!" he pointed to the hut by the river that their party had already searched. The Sergeant's rage came crashing faster than the waterfall in the distance.

"GO IN THAT HUT AND FIND THOSE DIRT BAGS. IN FACT, DON'T EVEN THINK OF LEAVING UNTIL YOU FIND THEM!!!"

The surge of threats was enough to send the search party into sprint and when everyone's attentions were away from the destroyed device, Kai pulled out a crimson cloth from his pocket. The crimson item had all the qualities of a handkerchief, despite the fact it was the last thing any sane person would bring to an active battlefield. He placed the crimson cloth on top of the device.

"Don't worry, at least your contributions won't be lost today," Kai said to himself. A minute passed and the crimson cloth shimmered once, in which he folded it back into his pocket. At this same moment shouting could be heard from the village hut. Boston's Army had found the rest of the villagers.

"That's right! Pull them all out, yep, all of them!"

One by one, the infantry pulled out bodies from a hidden crevice in the flooring, which led to a small dungeon. Sergeant Boston displayed all the shades of a sadist as he laughed throughout the exposé. He laughed particularly hard as his men pulled the Guyanese females by their curly hair. He encouraged his men when they struck the more fraught male members and he got his last fills of joy by gurgling racial remarks to the small children that were also pulled from the lower floor. When every last person had been captured by Boston's force, there were near to two hundred people; more individuals than the Sergeant had the puns, moreover, patience for. So, he ordered them all outside to line up on their knees. The apache helicopter was hovering over the village, guns reared, and flying inpatient circles.

"I want all of you to know one thing," Sergeant Boston took a patronising stroll along the line of Guyanese natives, "we took a day out of our normal operations to come check out this new tech we heard you have been using here. We come here and you greet us with what, fire? You greet us with fire? Why? We just wanted to share your toys."

"If you came why you say you came, you wouldn't have brought guns," replied one of the Guyanese men. This man had bristled hair as black as the Sergeant's heart and through his right eyebrow, was marked a slit inflicted by a past battle he had survived. As insubordination had been treated with harm throughout the captivity, a soldier motioned to punch the man, but Sergeant Boston intervened.

"WAIT soldier, stand down…" it was rare for the Sergeant to be on the giving end of pacification and so, everyone from American soil knew that he was going to wring every bit of amusement from the situation. As the leader of a mercenary army, the Sergeant was an occupational oppressor; he was used to talking down to people.

"And who might you be, except from the ugliest motherf*cker I have ever seen? And you should have seen my ex-wife,"

"I am Marcelo Sampson, the lead of this village. You are trespassing in a country where you do not belong. This is my people's technology, we built it. Having power does not give you the right to take it from us!" the man called Marcelo Sampson yelled.

"You're right. It does not give us the right, but it gives us the means." Sergeant Boston said. At those words, every infantry soldier perched their guns at the villagers in the line. Mothers put their children's heads into their chest and the armless villagers had no choice but to feed the soil their last bitter breaths. Marcelo Sampson remained straight, though he was shaking in fury.

"Jonathan Boston. I always doubted your ability as a leader, but this one takes the cake," this latest pitch of subordination, to the Sergeant's dismay, came from beside him. His son stepped into view next.

"Jonathan? It is Sergeant! Who do you think- "

"Shut up!" Kai fired blindly at the soldier who retaliated, "you can pay me to work with these morons, but you cannot pay me to lay my own grave. I have run some assessments on the device they had. Yes, it is cutting edge, a communications absorber – of all frequencies. You idiots fried the damn thing, but if we take it now, we can still replicate its design. You think if they gave this kind of technology to a rogue village that can barely defend itself, that they won't have more sophisticated bases elsewhere? By putting this thing offline they are probably sending reinforcements here now. I don't know about you, but I don't like being part of battles when we don't know who the enemy is. We need to take this device and the leader who we can get more information from. Forget about these innocent people, we will be wasting ammo... and time."

A tense silence followed requisition. The soldiers kept their guns forward and Kai slowly put his hand to the pocket his crimson handkerchief was in. The Sergeant released his gritted teeth.

"Are you f*ckers action figures? You heard him, put those guns down and head back to the carrier plane. Grab that ugly son of a b*tch and take that device-thingy with you." he threw a cigar packet at Kai once he reached for his last one. Kai gave an undetectable sigh. Having been around his father for seventeen of his twenty-three years of life meant that he, however little he wanted to, knew his father very well. A cigar was his ironic custom of blowing steam when he conceded defeat, especially in the arena of reason. An arena where logic had more power than firepower, and the very reason that Kai had cemented his place as the youngest head of operations, in the army's history.

"You lot go ahead, I am going to check their hideout for more tech,"

As the foot soldiers passed Kai, they gave him looks of abhor and nothing more. His rank as operations commander made him one of the few members who were authorized to display candor. Marcelo Sampson gave Kai Boston the sturdiest look of them all when they dragged the Guyanese leader away from his home. When the majority of the American invaders were some meters away, one of the younger Guyanese ladies approached Kai at a crawling speed, as if any haste would immediately revert his sense of mercy.

"There are no reinforcements. It is just us here. Our elders invented that machine, no one else."

"I know," said Kai.

"Is it our technology you want?" a villager said.

"Take this and go," a heavy set villager stuffed a small orb like object into Kai's hands, "this is an action gas grenade. This is what we used in the forest to take out some of your soldiers. It only paralyses for up to two hours if inhaled."

"This is not what I came for," this statement was true, but the fact that he rolled it within his crimson handkerchief meant he was going to take it home for study.

"Maybe, but you Americans need it. Not all battles must end with death. So, why did you let us live?"

"Because I am looking for someone and I know he's here," Kai's assertion came like a breeze from the Prism of the Center Wind. Two hundred heads spun faster than a whirligig. He watched as they turned to ask their neighbor 'how?!'

"The dungeon has two levels. Please do not harm him. That is my cousin," another Guyanese native came forward.

"I don't think he will. He's not like the others... who are you?"

"Never-Oppress-Man-Again." Kai stated, putting a periodic pause between each word. The Guyanese survivors were unblinking as the young commander descended to their dungeon.

Kai found the opening to the second and lower dungeon after some rummaging on the first. He had suspected that such a secretive and prospering community would have such provisions. Especially since his life had just as many layers. His blotched Korean life of old was one layer and the second was the path of retribution he had undertaken since. Kai's first foot touched the floor of the second dungeon and a head turned in its depths. The second dungeon was poorly lit bar a blitz of electric silver that came from its furthest corner. In that same corner a desk and a frantic collection of notes, theoretical, personal and otherwise were pinned to the stone walls. Some were titled 'Black Matter - theorem 234' and some were titled to various female names but were scrawled with such sentimentality that it could only be family. Kai stepped slowly toward the figure in the corner. He put the crimson cloth to his face and it shimmered. The silver light, bounced irregularly in the room. Slower than artificial light but more gripping than anything either man had seen before. This light pulsated from a sole bead, locked between the pincers of a Heron Industries microscope placement.

"If Madame Baelel has sent you, just get it over with," croaked a bearded Professor Jinx. His head remained bald and smooth, however. Despite the otherworldly prospect that he had at his desk, the Professors eyes widened when he saw the intruder come into view. Before his eyes, he saw a piece of crimson cloth change properties – from flimsy, to tungsten metal. Without touching it, the cloth had materialized into the distinctive helmet of the hero in the state he once knew.

`"You worked with Aaron Heron on the SuperSilver Project… you are going to tell me everything,"` came N.O.M.A.'s cryptic voice.

CHAPTER 2

Treasury

Unknown user: I can't believe how much information is on this thing.

NORU: Everything that I am permitted to store, I archive.

Unknown user: What is this file? Can you play me one of the recordings in the family LOGS inventory?

NORU: This had been locked by the main administrator.

Unknown user: Administrator huh, what are you – some sort of computer program?

NORU: I am not a program. I, too, am information. I have been coded with a voice module, so this is what you hear.

Unknown user: What else are you coded with.

NORU: Anything I am presented with. I am information.

Unknown user: By any chance, have you been coded with military grade weapons and communications technology?

NORU: (Processing automated response) HA - like I would tell you that.

Unknown user: Well- he clearly hasn't coded you with military grade security.

NORU: I can. If presented with the information.

Unknown user: How does the suit copy these things?

NORU: It is not the suit that copies. The suit itself is a copy of the unreleased prototype 'Vivogenesis' power suit made by the No-Ma-Ki tech company in Korea. This suit is made from tungsten and includes an internal emergency air bag and V-force raptor wing capability. This model was not released as it allegedly required too much processing power to run.

Unknown user: If the suit is a copy too, then where is all of the information stored?

NORU: It and myself and all other modules are contained within a matrix of infinite capacity. Upon contact, this matrix can copy the three dimensional information of non-organic matter and form it using the information. From my tests, the N.O.M.A. suit is the limits of the mass that the matrix can produce. It can store information of objects that are bigger, but cannot physically produce them.

Unknown user: So, how did he get this Matrix?

NORU: I am sorry, unknown user; I am not permitted to discuss that.

END OF TRANSMISSION

ELLAJ BROADCASTING STUDIOS

NEW ROYALE, NEW YORK

The Ellaj broadcasting studio cast a lime like limelight on their host: Starr Francis-Komet. The time between set up and live air was liminal and so a session of cosmetic sweepstakes was already underway. Many of the onset makeup artists tried their luck, approaching Starr with pomade brushes and brow pencils in hand, but when the young presenter politely refused them, the only thing they were left to draw were unflattered faces of their own. Starr remained bare face throughout the pre-show preparation and when the studio lights withered at last, she sat straight, ready to deliver a bare faced truth.

"Good evening, my name is Starr Francis-Komet and welcome to my weekly show '*Starrting Change*'. The focus of today's show is a subject called '*Treasury*'. You probably have begun to hear this word being used in some national debates, but for all those who do not know, I will explain. '*Treasury*' is a term that relates to state organisations that infiltrate or exploit less established communities for resources, technology or information. The act of '*Treasury*' seemingly goes unpublicized as it is often masqueraded as an act of war or an operation against terrorism. '*Treasury*' has been going on for longer than you and I may think. And this key missing part of our documented history is because of successful indoctrination, of which our safety has said been supposedly prioritised. Fear has often been used as justification and

16

generations of our country have swallowed this without question. It is pretty much America's taboo, and I really think it is important to have discussions about powerful nations abusing their force. The current debates about '*Treasury*', I hope, will begin to protect less established communities from being exploited and shed light more on oppressive practices. The rise of non-governmental development in information technology and the subsequent trials for it to remain independent and unsolicited is becoming a growing discussion in a field that has been called techno-politics. We are starting to see all types of movements start from this. Mainstream media are only now starting to treat this as news worthy and licensing agencies are beginning to appear, with intentions to regulate the use of these breakthrough technologies. Every country has different rules for the authorization of certain weapon and defense technologies, but these licensing and defense authorities will make sure that unmonitored parties do not come from this," Starr took a deep breath followed by a long intake of her bottled water. Along with her armchair, the set was filled with a corner desk, and multiple socioeconomic books which read titles ranging from the common to the near radical. Countless scattered sheets of paper were like leaves from this branch of research. She had penned more words than her screen time would permit, and so she neatly placed her drink to the desk once again. Alongside the contents of the bottle, her intensity for the topic watered down somewhat.

"It is important that the topic of '*treasury*' continues to be recognised as a current issue. Misinformation is just as much of a weapon than any gun. For all we know, many of the greatest breakthroughs in recent history may have been taken from unaccredited and unnamed individuals of whom we may never know. If we dim the lights of the pioneers of this world, no matter which nation, religion or cause they serve, we risk nullifying the true potential of what the human race can achieve. If we let the dictatorship of the strongest nations assume the speed of our advancements, I'm afraid that there will be a time that we halt. When breakthrough communities and persons are exploited of their technology, the abusive nations may benefit in the short term, but humanity loses in the long term. When the foundations of work are destroyed, so are more possibilities of what those pioneering minds and peoples could offer. '*Treasury*' is a counterproductive form of actions fueled by greed for marketing of technology companies. Where do we begin to turn back the pages of our history book and evaluate, seriously evaluate, the adverse effects on the techno-political climate over the last few decades. Can we reach a point in our world that knowledge is shared and celebrated, not feared and branded under exclusivity? Of course, we cannot change the past, but we can for the future, strive for difference – as always, thank you for listening to my words my loyal Starr-Gazers. Now, we're going to answer a few fan questions from my blog, that will be continued on the podcast segment of this show," Starr continued to finish her brief free verse segment whilst the studio team behind the cameras set into motion the conclusion of her sequence. The lime like limelight's lost their zest and transformed into a frosty blue glare. The scene team and the onset make-up artists lifted their heels from the ground, as if ready to burst from their starting blocks. Starr's last words of information became drowned out by Ellaj's Studios signature theme tune and after it had reached the heights of its melody, the studio cameras swung to the second panel which contained their news team. The cut and clean presenters broke into their usual guises and introduced the watching audiences to America's latest success - Boston's Army's counter-terrorism efforts in South America.

Boston's Base (Operations room)

Heavens Conquest, Indiana

A Caucasian male found himself doing a light jog down one of Boston's Bases long corridors. His appearance suggested he was on the declining spectrum of the twenties, and despite working for an army, his fitness level did no favours to better this suggestion. The looming length of the corridor gave the illusion that the door was closer than it was, and so when the man finally reached the door, he had paths of sweat through his buzz cut and his operations officer uniform had been rendered marshy, especially at the underside of his arms.

KNOCK! KNOCK! KNOCK!

"Who is it?"

"C'mon man you know it's me, open up,"

"I don't know anything,"

"Well open the flap!"

"Name?"

"Why do you always do this...?"

"Name?"

"Henry!"

"Henry who?"

"Uh, geez I don't know. How about the Henry you work with every day?"

An eye level, iron shutter slid open – the only thing separating the corridor from the room beyond the door. Oriental shaped eyes studied the surroundings before resting on the frustrated (and noticeably sweaty) inquirer. The iron shutter slid shut once again and without a word, the door to the operations room opened. What the room lacked in breadth, it made up for in width, as it housed enough space for a panel of operators to attend the elongated switchboard, but not much else. Underneath the desk were food bins and in the far right corner, a crimson backpack. The wall was a spider web of interconnected screens, feeding live camera footage from every conceivable part of their military base. Patrolling soldiers and watchtower scouts could be seen glancing toward the camera's every so often, in knowledge that they were being overseen by the operations team. Lastly, the operations room had red, hellish lighting and from within it, the face of Kai Boston was crossed with glee, having pressed his colleague into following protocol for the untold time.

"You are a jerk, you know that right?" Henry, who was carrying a newspaper, slouched into the narrowed room before taking a seat on one of the several wheeled chairs. He was also quick to notice that Henry was not the only intruder, as he brought a strong stream of biological odour with him.

"It's been said. Just following protocol," Kai sniffed, "I hope you know we have shower units on site?"

"Like you care about protocol," Henry tossed the folded newspaper into Kai's lap. Before he could even spread the newspaper, the operations leader was visibly irked.

"Why the f*ck have you given me this. You know I don't follow the news,"

"You are gonna' wanna' see this,"

"If you are not going to stay to do work, then just leave," Kai returned the newspaper with one disinterested swing of his thin hand.

"Stop being so stubborn, it's about the army's recent mission in Guyana," this latest sentence struck a chord because upon returning the paper, Henry was met with accord. When he read the headline, the expression of the operations leader stretched tighter than his cordovan leather boots:

Young & Oliver Trent Times

Boston's Base: unsung heroes of our country

Less than forty-eight hours ago, the private military army based in the city of Heavens Conquest, Indiana, ran a covert operation in South America. This operation was with the intent to disarm the country of Guyana who were armed with potentially compromising weapons. This mission was a resounding success, with the army able to single handedly infiltrate and take away these technologies with minimal collateral damage. Due to Sergeant Boston's courageous commitment to national defense, Boston's Base has been nominated for an Avali Peace Prize, which the annual ceremony takes place this autumn in Italy. This marks a tremendous year for the United States as renowned scientist and CEO Aaron Heron has also been slated as a contender for the Avali Science Prize, despite being missing still. The federal investigations bureaus are still trying to locate Mr. Heron, but until then I am sure Boston's Base will be issuing a lot of medals in celebration.

When his eyes had left the last words of the headline, even the red glow of the room could not disguise his fire.

"My friend, the Avali peace prize? Do you know what that means? Our salary is going up – especially yours! You coordinated everything- "

"Shut up, Henry – please," Kai's hands were clamped together, the newspaper between them.

"What's wrong with you man, its good news?"

"It's bullsh*t, it is all bullsh*t. A Peace prize? The mission couldn't be further from that."

"But we disarmed their dangerous weapons?"

"You were not there. During our training, I don't remember being taught that a sophisticated signal absorber classifies as a dangerous weapon. Don't believe everything you read,"

"You organised it. Why did you take our army there then?" Their eye contact faltered from Kai's side. His head knelt at the sword of the question.

KNOCK! KNOCK! KNOCK!

Still eyeing Kai some, Henry rose to open the door. To his dismay, the awaiting guests were none other than Sergeant Boston himself and a tall, knobbly, bearded man in a recruit uniform.

"I've smelt corpses better than this place," the Sergeant attacked his own nose with a finger. Henry folded his arms as far inward as he could.

"Ladies, this is the newest member of the operations team: Liam Laverton," he then faced the tall, pink faced man himself, "as you can see it is a small team. If the smell of this sty does not drive you away, the actual job will. It's not for everyone but with your background you should be at home," he ended by thumping Liam proudly on the back, but the only thing this encouraged was meek splutters of gratitude.

"Thank you for the opportunity Sergeant, seriously."

"You won't be thanking me once you have got to meet my joy of a son. He's the leader of operations and will be the one taking you through induction,"

"Hey," said Liam. Kai did not respond. For all he cared, the greeting could exist forever without his acknowledgement. Nothing of their first meet told him that he would fare better than the previous recruits who tried out for a place on the operations team. Just from his appearance, Kai could see that the man named Liam Laverton did not pay attention to details. His long brown hair was gelled inconsistently and in Kai's honest opinion, looked like more like a wet mop that had been thrown onto his head. Also, Liam Laverton's beard and moustache had been trimmed to different levels, making it look like he had fight with his barber. Appearance aside, however, certain core skills were needed: decision making, tactical IQ and communications intelligence. He could see that the new recruit was weaved in insecurity just by the way he wrapped his hands each other. The remaining core skills could not be deciphered from face value, but he assumed the recruit must compensate in the two remaining areas, given he was being personally recommended by his father. Either way, Kai was one interrogation away from finding out himself. The Sergeant adjusted his belt before proclaiming his exit.

"Good luck rookie," he pointed a single finger to his son, "I want you to be at the Avali Peace Prize ceremony. You will be accepting the prize for the army," With that, the Sergeant began his wide stride back down the single hallway that seemed to have no end.

"I'm gonna' go too," Henry doused the room with a nearby can of scented aerosol as he made way for the door.

"Don't worry about the induction, he practically runs the place by himself anyway," Henry whispered to Liam Laverton as he passed him. When Henry had left, Kai and the new recruit were left alone.

Liam, the new recruit, took a seat in Henry's damp chair and was forced to endure the combined pressures of a stagnant silence, a pair of slanted eyes studying him and the red glare of the rooms lights, which seemed to make things increasingly heated. The recruit decided that the cool use of humor could ice everything over.

"It's funny; I've never had a boss who was younger than me,"

"And I've never heard of a new recruit who is nearing retirement," said Kai, almost immediately. He watched as the recruit did not retaliate to the scathing insult, but instead wrapped himself with it, acceptingly, as if it was a scarf. Liam proceeded warmly,

"Yeah, I am not the man I used to be but I've still got a lot left to give that's for sure,"

"Why us?"

"I will tell you one thing young man. This world is not what it seems. There are a lot of curtains, a lot of facades. I've worked in many sectors of government intelligence and all I've seen in my life are agendas. Intentions, but no action. Seeing this all your life, it's frustrating. Especially when you know things that should be different. If Sergeant Boston is helping to pull down these curtains, then I am all in to help."

"For all you know, Boston's Base could just another regime helping the façade," Kai suggested, half hoping this would deter the recruit.

"Really? This army has just been nominated for an Avali Peace Prize. There is no place more honorable to spend my last few working years,"

"How old are you?" Kai reached for the crimson backpack underneath his desk and from it, he pulled a tablet device that he began operating with intuitive strokes of his index finger.

"I might look a bit older, but I'm only forty," Liam said.

"You are younger than the Sergeant; you still have more than two decades to work if you wanted."

"The government jobs paid well," Liam continued to revolve his hands.

"I can see that. You used to be advisor for some foreign embassies. Handwritten references from the senators of Russia and India themselves. Who would have thought you were such a big deal," with genuine impress, Kai scrolled through Liam Laverton's resume that was now uploaded onto his tablet.

"How did you get that? That is not the resume I applied with?"

"Err, the internet," Kai lied, still waving his finger through Liam's long list of accomplishments in the field of communications and human relations. He would never vocalize it, but it even surpassed his own. Kai found some redemption in the fact that even though Liam Laverton was overqualified; he would still be underneath him in the status quo.

"I don't say this often, but I am impressed," said the bittersweet leader.

"Thank you, Mr. Boston,"

"Call me Kai, as long as you are in my team that is," Kai gave his seal of approval in the form of an outstretched hand. When Liam gratefully reciprocated the gesture, Kai was mildly surprised how cold his touch was, given how warm his mannerisms were.

"Any questions?" asked Kai.

N.O.M.A.   L.K. BROOKS-SIMPSON

"I would just like to know where the other departments are, storage and utilities – stuff like that,"

"I have already emailed a password encrypted induction pack to your email. It has maps, descriptions of every sector. Salary, etcetera."

"Oh wow. Quick-"

"Anything else?"

"If I get here early, how do I get into this room? Do I get a set of keys?"

"There are only one set of keys to the operations room," Kai pulled out a thin necklace from underneath his jumper, of which a single key dangled from its end, "this key locks the door from both the inside and the outside. Fortunately, you don't have to worry about getting in, there will never be a time that I'm not here while you are working. Just give the door a knock; state your name and I might open the door. Depending on my mood," Liam chortled at the end of Kai's words.

"Depending on my mood – love that."

"I'm being serious," Kai did not return an inch of amusement, "If I do not open the door then please work from the radio offices upstairs, cos' I'm probably busy with something important."

"Oh..."

"Anything else?"

"That's a nice bag you got under there," Liam peered over Kai's knee which was partially blocking his view. Kai's first instinct was to block his view completely, however, he managed to embrace restraint.

"Oh-oh that thing? Yeah, it's my work bag. Take it with me sometimes."

26

"Where'd you get it from, sure one of my kids wanted something similar," Liam's lips pursed through his beard as he tried to recollect.

"I can't remember. I'm sure I got it during one our missions to Europe, years ago," Kai had inched ever so slightly between the view of the recruit and his backpack and thankfully for him, the knobbly recruit got to his feet.

"Well, if that is all I have got to head off. Gotta' get home and tell the family the good news,"

"You do that sir, you do that," Kai rotated his chair half a circle, but he was not met with the shut of the door, only another question.

"Aren't you coming? Its late, I'm sure your mother or other half is waiting?"

"My mother has passed. I don't have time for another half and as the media has probably told you hundreds of times, me and my father don't exactly have the best of relationships. I'm leaving soon, just need to finish a few things,"

"A young man with no perceivable loved ones. That's a bit sad,"

"I prefer it that way,"

"With an Avali Peace Prize coming I would shoot my shot with that hot presenter at America's Interest – what's her name Starr? All right, all right I'm going. You need to lighten up kid..."

Kai watched his company exit until the steel door was shut in place. He could not truly relax until he was alone. Having a capable member of the team was just as much as of an advantage as it was a drawback. He would now have to be even more discreet about operating his double life as Kai Boston and N.O.M.A. - watcher of Heavens Conquest. Kai blew air upwards before grabbing his backpack. Upon contact it melted from its shape and in several seconds that resembled an invisible computer animator modifying an object, it had stretched into a thick sleeping bag. The now formed sleeping bag shed some of its matter to form a feathery, crimson pillow. The operations commander relieved himself of his uniform until he had, ironically, gone commando. When he pulled himself into a comfortable position in his sleeping bag, he touched some buttons on this tablet until it synchronised with the network of screens on the room's walls. The screens blinked crimson and shortly after, his favourite television programmes were on play; mixed martial arts championships were playing on one half of the wall, whilst K-movies played on the other. With little effort, Kai had turned the operations room into both an entertainment booth and sophisticated communications hub – what he considered home. Both the screens and satellites were now an extension of his neural network; his eyes and ears so to speak. He had the majority of the army's outbound signals at hand and the camera feeds on the streets of Heavens Conquest at his fingers. He was the operator of the base, but the oculate for the city.

CHAPTER 3

Helle Bushida

NORU: Do you intend to return me to my compartment in the N.O.M.A. suit? I belong there.

Unknown user: Ugh, you're still talking. How long do your batteries last?

NORU: I am integrated with the information of self-sustaining power sources. When I am not receiving energy from our pilot satellite, then I convert kinetic energy into fuel, to power me.

Unknown user: He has a satellite too... kinda cool.

NORU: My kinetic sensors also noted that you travel between the cities of Heavens Conquest and Signot a lot.

Unknown user: Yeah, I have business in both cities... so?

NORU: It would be more efficient to relocate to just one place. I estimate that you would reduce travel by 86 miles a week. You could save 4 hours and 36 minutes. Also you could almost reduce those 36 minutes completely if you stop arguing with other humans.

Unknown user: A step counter? At least you can do something useful.

NORU: You are misinformed, I am designed solely to be useful.

Unknown user: Well tell me something useful then. Something even N.O.M.A. doesn't know.

NORU: (Processing) - there was a survey conducted outside of the United States asking what the capital of Indiana was. An overwhelming 84% believed it to be Signot, due to its recent industrialization and tourist appeal. 10% said they don't know and only 4.6% answered correctly: Heavens Conquest.

Unknown user: To be honest, back when I lived in Dallas, I probably wouldn't have known that either.

NORU: The city of Heavens Conquest has a rich history since becoming the state capital in the year 1782. Heavens Conquest is home to the fourth longest highway in Midwestern America - it connects both Signot, Babil City and the Indiana dunes. You could also travel 2/5th's of this highway with the time you spend commuting in a week. You could travel 1/8th of the highway with the time you spend arguing.

Unknown user: Ha-ha...

NORU: Heavens Conquests popular locale, 'The Venia Strip' once held one of the most notorious casinos back in the 1970's. It was shut down when supposed mafia activity was being investigated by state police. When the CIA got involved, this period of no business caused the owners to go bankrupt. Heavens conquest is also home to the Indiana's only Ministry buildings, of which the Mayor of Indiana works from. Because Heavens Conquest has been the home of the Mayors, it has a rich political history. Politicians that started in this cities ministry have gone on to many executive and legislative positions in other states.

Unknown user: Yeah and left Indiana to deal with its own problems.

NORU: Even though Indiana has been going through a depression during the last decade, Heavens Conquest has been relatively unaffected. Over the last three years Heavens Conquest has seen the resignation of eleven major ministry members who were posed to introduce ineffective public policies.

Unknown user: I know. I've seen it with my own eyes, he has been watching over us.

NORU: Always watching. Since possession of the suit and integration of my modules, I have acquired a lot of information. He told me that none of the information is effective, unless we can help others. So that is my grand objective; to help.

END OF TRANSMISSION

BOSTON'S BASE (INTERNATIONAL DETAINMENT UNIT)

HEAVENS CONQUEST, INDIANA

The prospect of becoming public figures put a rift in usual protocol at Boston's Base. Men who were extensively trained for military excellence would be found mulling over the copious details that came with a ceremony as prestigious as the *Avali Awards.* Topics such as entrée's, ensemble and etiquette had many of the employees excitable, if not enlightened to stray from en brosse hairstyles for once in their life. The good air around the base even extended to the Sergeant who, despite his deplorability in the eyes of most, gifted his longest serving soldiers celebratory leave in preparation for the event. He hung flaunting banners the shade of 'envy me' green, from the base's watchtowers. Towers that were deliberately designed to be seen from main hub of the city and if the Sergeant could have his way, the streets of Heavens Conquest would be draped in green also. The Sergeant did not step where his authority did not extend, but with spirits so high, he decided to at least rule the skies. Shortly after the news, a blimp advertising their Avali Peace Prize nomination could be seen floating gloatingly above the city. These dedicated efforts came at the back of the armies public shaming for losing Aaron Heron's sun suit, and not only was Boston's boastful display proof that boosterism was a fruitful avenue for exposure, but also a necessary step forward according to their public relations team. Public perception was much like clearing debt; once affections and dues were paid, one could do little wrong. In a week that included a sweep of envy-me green banners, a feature in GAS magazine (the biggest lifestyle magazine in North America) and a boisterous blimp that could swing heads all the way from the city of Signot, the members of Boston Base found out the true power of national politics. Commendation from the right societies could grant them an invincibility even their advanced arms could not provide; reverence. Whilst most of America was ready to leave Aaron Heron's missing suit in the book of 2012, one man refused to continue the story without answers. Kai Boston studied this page every day. He tried to figure how it fitted in with the larger story and he also studied it in more detail than any before him. He unearthed every connotation he could, from every sentence it served. He even ripped a page from its rightful place in the book for further evaluation. He came to know the page as much as its contents would allow and so his observations progressed to the dimensions of the page. How many words its length could hold. The terseness of its paper. Whether the words held their meaning in different conditions; say, a flame to the edge of the parchment. A douse underneath water. It was a durable page. For a page it was surprisingly thick and for a page it was surprisingly short on words.

"I don't know why you wear a mask, I have seen your face already," said Marcelo Sampson, leader of the Sharpa Rainforest village. Though Kai wore his black half mask, the underside to his N.O.M.A. suit, it was Marcelo who looked besides himself. Compared to their encounter in Guyana, the leader had shed several pounds and looked generally underfed. Kai rolled a loaf of bread toward the two occupants of the unit, Marcelo and Professor Noel Jinx, who was awake, but slumped beside him.

"And if you tell anyone then guess who is signing you off as an incompliant captive?" Kai held three separate papers in his hands and he fed them between each gap that separated his fingers.

"Young man, we both know I have done nothing wrong. You will send me away but in turn, your soul will rot," Marcelo growled.

"You will wish you'd rot first, locked up in Hallows Island with those madmen. Have you ever seen a maximum security prison before? Consider this as luxury. Trust me," Kai pointed to the small grey room, which was largely empty, aside from its toilet cubicle and two bed plans.

"The only reason I am here is to get information from him. I want to know everything he knows about Aaron Heron and the SuperSilver project," Kai's mask moved, but his eyes were tagged on the Professor.

"I swear to my family, if I knew what you wanted to know, I would have told you by now! None of this is worth it," Marcelo's eyelids flexed outwards until they could not be seen. Tunnels of frustrated capillaries could be seen on the whites of his eyes.

"I know," Kai agreed.

"Then why burn the man's research? Do you know how much important discoveries are on there?"

"Because I don't like to repeat myself. His SuperSilver discovery has caused something I have never seen before, something supernatural. There are super humans running around our cities and if there are more things like that, that he has been working on, I need to know. He saw how many people the Spectre killed. I can't afford to take the chance of people being in danger like that again. But he clearly can – he's going to just watch all of his hard work burn away. A page at a time," with a flick, a lighter ignited in his other hand, and Kai slowly teased a flame to the edge of the first piece of paper. The way Marcelo lunged from his seat, a neutral onlooker would assume either the heat somehow transported to the bottom of his chair or that the masked man was to burn his only claim to livelihood. With martial reflexes, Kai had swapped out a lighter in place of stun gun.

"I would sit the f*ck down if I were you, this is a military grade taser – you won't make it to the cubicle," Marcelo heeded the warning by taking a slouched seat beside his countryman who did not even raise a head.

"Cousin, just tell the young man what he wants. This is your life work," Marcelo physically shook the Professor by the shoulders, but this did not instill any urgency whatsoever. Noel Jinx's' leant head was only helped to the other side by the movement. Kai truly did not understand the depth of the information he was seeking, especially, if it could deter a former scientific professional. Someone who had sworn years of study and research to sharing information with the world. Stranger still was that Professor Jinx, on internet descriptions of his live lectures, was described as a vocal lecturer, but the man he was saw in front of him nothing more than an inconsolable mute. These peculiar equations of Jinx' personality did not add up whatsoever and for someone who predicated their plans on as much information as possible, Kai was facing a blank wall in both regards. His curiosity burned brighter than ever and as a result, the lighter flicked on again. A teasing flame reared its orange head. Only when flame met paper did a pair of eyes look upwards. Even through the Professors impassivity, he could see disheartenment. Disheartenment when a man who had lost everything, slowly but surely, lost the last things he had left, his research papers. Kai was as crafty as the Professor was unwilling to cooperate. Jinx had not spoken a single world since being discovered, Kai on the other hand, though having inherited his father's irritability, was compelled by circumspect. A quality he remembered his Korean village used to reiterate. For this reason only, the research papers were mostly in full and were not a pile of cinders on the detainment unit floor. Just as the flame had claimed the tail of the page, Kai suddenly became distracted from his task. Soon enough, he withdrew a cellular device from his chest pocket, waved the flame from existence (perhaps more eagerly than he let on) and returned the scorched contents to his pocket, right beside his crimson handkerchief.

"Looks like some divine intervention has come your way professor," came his masked words, "I will get my information sooner or later so I advise to start speaking soon and save what you can."

Marcelo Sampson was the latest occupant to lean their head. Kai imagined Marcelo felt like a living hangman; strung between the words his cousin would not speak and words of research that was being sacrificed as a result. As Kai made to leave, the professor spoke his first words and they came in a dry croak,

"You wouldn't be able to handle the truth." Kai stopped in his tracks, but he did not pivot.

"With all due respect Professor, there is not much I cannot handle," he began, "by the way your electrolyte levels are low. Ask the detainment officers for a man called Henry Sammis in the operations team. He will bring you more food and supplements," with another glance at his cell phone, the two prisoners were left alone in the cold clutches of captivity.

Boston's Base was categorised as an establishment in the city of Heaven's Conquest and was often said to be based in the outskirts of the capital. However, the Base was in fact a notable collection of the mass called the Indiana dunes. These dunes stretched from the feet of Heaven's Conquest all the way to its neighbour Babil City, then to the west of Indiana. The dunes were comprised with mostly patches of forestry that had managed to survive the aridity, followed by huge metal and concrete remains from Indiana's industrialization, buried under decade's worth of sandstorms. Aside from a few small beach towns and N.O.M.A.'s secret bunker (named bunker 55 - confinement of the super villain Spectre), the dune was largely neglected. A route to pass through at most. Boston's Base was the dunes sole sandcastle so to speak, meticulously constructed and avidly defended.

An armoured vehicle approached from the direction of the base and while the dunes carpets tried to deter it with swift inclines, swifter winds and shifts in traction, the large four by four kept on track until it stopped by a lone bystander in the middle of the desert. The person standing was a woman and the most noticeable thing about the lady was the white tae kwon do uniform that she was wearing; an oasis in the sands. The second, was her neck; extremely long and the passageway leading to spar ready shoulder blades and a fitness, fit frame. The woman looked youthful from the face and her eyes slanted north. The east of Asia could be seen in her features, alongside the breezy flair of downtown Indiana. When the armoured car came to a halt, a smile dawned west of her mouth.

"Nice toy, did Daddy let you borrow it?"

"Shut up and get in – or walk," Kai greeted her. When she climbed in, Kai continued progress in the same direction, in other words, toward the capital. The young lady angled her reflection into the door mirror nearest her as she shaped her curly, pixie styled haircut. Midway during this session, she stopped completely and decided to lay commentary for the silent journey. The conversation ricocheted from one another and the only thing more familiar than their discourse was Kai's progress toward the city.

"If you hate working at the army so much, why don't you just leave?"

"I can't just leave, Helle. I'm needed there."

"What about what you need? The dojo is what makes you happy,"

"I make time for it,"

"Barely, you didn't even have time to put your gi on today,"

"I'll do that when we get there. No matter what you say, I'm staying at the base,"

"You know I'm right. You just have too much pride to leave cos' that would be admitting I'm right,"

"I wish things were like that,"

"Anyway, I'm not trying to stress you out more. Just looking out for your stubborn ass,"

"I know. I know,"

"For the record I know you wouldn't have let me walk Kai,"

"You don't know me as well as you think you do girl,"

Helle Bushida was both Kai's confidant and weakness. Despite being the only person who had managed to navigate the maze that was his mulish ways, there was only so far he would allow a person to know him. Helle knew Kai Boston extremely well, perhaps better than his own army colleagues, but when it came to his alter ego N.O.M.A., she had not the faintest suspicion. Helle was none the wiser to what Kai truly represented and for this very reason, in his eyes, she was his only weakness. Since meeting two years ago at their dojo, he had come to learn that she was more than capable of protecting herself, however, even the strongest warrior could not protect themselves from a threat that they did not know was coming. This was one of the reasons that N.O.M.A. wore the mask and preached the importance of anonymity like gospel.

"I've never asked you this," Kai began, "but why did you join the dojo in the first place? It's not exactly close to Babil city?"

"Mattias Sensei is one of the best teachers of martial arts in the entire world. I would travel downstate for the classes if that's where he was holding them," Helle declared. There was a Californian twang to her accent, confirmation that she had not lived her entire life in Indiana, at the same time, her handle on the Indianan discourse, was evidence that she had lived most of her life in the state.

"So that's why you joined, just for him?"

"No," there was a noticeable slow in her sentences now, "seven years ago, my brother was killed by the Bulgarian Conglomerate, just for being a witness to one of their crimes. A witness. My brother was in the wrong place at the wrong time and the man they call Maximov sent men to kill him in cold blood. Mattias Sensei is one of the best and I will learn from nothing less than. I know that if my brother was still here, he'd want me to know how to defend myself. That's all. Defend myself and live a good life," when Helle had finished she was wearing a scowl so intense, Kai thought twice about asking further. Just as he had committed himself to the silence, further corroboration came his way,

"Maybe next time don't ask questions you don't want the answer to."

"I don't know why Sensei thinks my attitude stinks, he should really hear you outside of dojo sometimes,"

"Yours does, you think you are better than everyone else there. You are not there to improve, just to show you're the best," said Helle.

"I am the best," Kai nodded to himself.

"Not better than Mattias Sensei,"

"Do you truly believe that?" Kai eyed his passenger and watched her exhale a doubtful breath of air, before reaching for the instruments of the armoured vehicle.

"Does the army let you guys listen to music in these things," crisp radio waves eventually formed intelligible sounds, and to the dismay of the listeners, it was breathless commentary:

"Breaking News! A crazy scene is currently taking place at Heaven Conquest's ministry house. As crazy as it sounds, a man in a suit and golden mask has taken three politicians hostage on the buildings third floor balcony and seems to be auctioning, yes auctioning, who he will throw from it. I use the word auctioning because this masked man has a crowd of protesters and fans at the steps of the ministry building cheering and jeering at his words. He is exposing the politician's crime to the crowd and asking them who he should execute. It is almost like a pantomime, it is absurd! There are minimal police currently at the scene because all of the major roads have been blocked off by armed men. Whatever this spectacle is, it has been clearly coordinated some time before this all began. The man in the mask is carrying some sort of firearm but has not used it yet. We will stay live at the scene for further updates, but please stay well clear of the ministry square and by any means do not join the crowd of people encouraging this terrorist scene. There have been no sightings of N.O.M.A. or our own cities army, but given the sensitive state of the situation, we can only hope that this situation is resolved without any casualties."

Kai slammed on the brakes.

"I gotta' go back to the base. Our army might be on call if the situation gets worse,"

"You're going to make me walk aren't you?" Helle simplified. Kai fumbled the word 'yes' in his head for some seconds, in full knowledge that speaking it would probably bring about one of her brief spells of seasonal loathing.

"I can't believe this d!ckhead is going to make me walk," Helle ejected herself from the vehicle and closed the door with such force that he felt the entire four by four jolt.

"Don't slam doors! It's a car, not a tank!" Kai retorted at a yell, however, his point was only met by the point of her middle finger as she walked away.

"An update live from the terrorist scene at the ministry building. The man has referred to himself as Midas."

Kai Boston whipped the military car with such force that the U-turn could have had an exclamation mark. As he feigned his journey back towards the base, he reached for his crimson backpack in the backseat.

"Finally, a real job to do," he said to himself.

CHAPTER 4

Midas

Ministry Buildings

Heavens Conquest, Indiana

"What we have here are three living examples of the type of people your parents warned you about. You know, the kind of people who say they want the best for you but really they don't. Is it a bit insensitive to say 'living example' right now?" the mouth of a golden plated revolver kissed the temple of all three kneeled and tied politicians. The politicians whimpered as much as their gagged, mouth ties would allow. Their whimpers were induced as much as from the fear of a fatal gunshot to the head as from the idea of their forty foot fall – if pushed. Even a fatal gunshot to the head seemed a better path than facing the arbitrary actions of their histrionic hostage-taker.

"What was that Linda? Can I call you Linzy actually?" the man named Midas knelt beside the only female captive, and by the wetness around her eyes, the most distraught. Muffled shrieks came from the middle-aged lady as the mask of Midas entered her view.

"You're not here against your will, if you want to go just say so," said Midas. The woman nodded profusely.

"You want to stay Linzy?" he rested his forearms on his long knees and angled his head in sally. She then shook her head so fast her hair whipped her shoulders.

"Sure you can stay," the captor began, "but least you and good Blake could do is clear up the rumours about Sallie Mae first, eh?" the woman buried her face as far into her shoulder as she could, when she realised that she was being toyed with. The captor stood again, and he was a lanky figure. He wore thin, stitched leather gloves; with the propensity of avoiding forensic entities. The rest of his outfit was the product of fine stitch work and eighteenth-century design. He had tailored trousers and a baggy blazer that fell to his quadriceps. Both of these items were the colour of washed black; a shade of their former selves. He stood in patent leather, half heel boots which were Socrates approved, as they laid the foundations of his pioneering, six-foot one frame. Even with their exclusion he was a rather tall human. A contracted and consequently, creased, pale blouse shirt sat underneath his tired blazer. The collar of this blouse faced the skies and tied around it was a black, silk ribbon. The captor's face was hidden behind a mask, but the mask was the furthest thing from ubiquitous. The mask was shaped for the masquerade, however, the metal domino had been forged with such realism, it was if it the face had belonged to a human, lost in their golden glory. Its nose, lips and brows were shaped with sadness but the smile was crass and unforgettable. Its material was bold, having the quality of twenty four carat gold and the mask stayed put across the face of the man by two single clasps, wrapped around his bald crown. Within Midas' touch was his trusted golden revolver; equally as pure according to the twenty-four carat signet by the barrel. Three slits within the mask ensured ventilation for its wearer; thin, pink lips could be just about be seen by the mouth and seedy, attentive eyes were trapped behind the golden eyelets.

"Do you see that?" Midas tapped the revolver on the captive he was addressing: a greying, Caucasian man and the second in line, "the people below want some – what do we call it – compensation," despite the predicament, the man made several intonations through his gag, the sounds of reason.

"Oh, Blake Nigel. You are such a sweet talker. Unfortunately, I think the people feel differently," Midas clutched the politician by his blazer neck and leant him dangerously forward over the edge of the balcony. From the third floor of the ministry building, the products of political commodity could be seen; crowds of contest on the ministry steps, Bolivian blockades on the main road and inner city police plotting by the side streets.

"Please just let us go. We will give you whatever you want, just name it," murmured the third politician in line. Midas, who still had the second politician leant over the balcony, turned toward the audible hostage as if he had interrupted a father showing his son a view for the first time. Midas' showed no such compassion when he let Blake Nigel drop to his peril, just so he could address the third hostage. He was so focused on the outspoken hostage in fact, that he did not notice the sound of a metallic swoop from outside. Midas had the symphony of Linda's cries and the percussion of the crowd's screams, to lay his next words.

"And, and who told you that you could remove your mouth tie,"

"I am tied by the hands, how could I remove it? You just did not tie it that tight?"

"Are you saying I'm bad at my job?" Midas said in a high pitch.

"What? No, no, - sir I'm saying-" exclaimed the chubby politician as best as he could make out.

"I have the men of that stubborn Bolivian drug lord at my beckon. I have locked off the main roads of the central district. The police are unable to get to the scene and I have single handedly infiltrated the ministry building, have three of Heavens Conquests most controversial politicians on their knees in front of national television – and you are telling me I'm bad at my job?"

"No I – I never meant – I don't know what you're saying,"

"Well there were three politicians, I guess there's two now... technically,"

"Listen, just tell me what you want, sir, just let us go. Me at least!" the man spluttered as the gag slipped further into his mouth. A flat, stormy laugh came from the golden mask.

"If you think you can bribe a man like me then you are even more stupid than I thought. I make my own fortune," Midas, turned to the balcony, "the only thing I want is for my final guest to arrive, and by the looks of things, he should be here soon."

SWOOSH!

The police provisions in a nearby alleyway flinched when a crimson figure landed next to them. When the figure settled it was Heavens Conquests own vigilante: N.O.M.A., with the quivering politician, Blake Nigel in his arms. The different and specific, compartments of the suit flexed from their fittings as he moved. His arced helmet was composed of a visor tinted the shade grey and faintly engrained with a telemetric panel which displayed either an overview of the suit's essential functions, or a live telegram of previously recorded footage. The body of the suit had a sleek but bulked design and was trimmed with minimal lines of grey along its finer locations; the lane through the oblique's and the folds that made its fingers. The power engineered functions were enunciated by the faint hum from within its shell. Its shell was a plexus of sectioned crimson plates that animated the suit with even the slightest movement, giving the impression that he was a tungsten gargoyle that had been brought to live a crimson existence. His insignia, a triple lined rhombus, was visible at his chest, and right below it a circular chunk of crimson was missing. Leaving the black mesh of his under suit exposed. The suit, as if aware of this weak spot itself, shifted its compartments until that chunk was covered in tungsten once again and the metal by his right hand exposed itself in its place. Every single member of the discreet Indiana police unit turned to look at him. The suit was incomparable; words could only capture so much of its wonder and memory could maintain its magnetism for only so long. Some of the members could be seen taking pictures on their mobile phone.

"You should be used to flying, with all that student loan money you've been sitting on." When N.O.M.A. released the politician to ground, one of the policemen escorted Blake Nigel to safety. A lead cop (stated by her badge title) peered around the corner, leading to the incident at the ministry houses, before addressing the suited saviour.

"I hope you know that vigilantism is not a lawful in this state,"

"Technically, it is not illegal either. And I hope you know that you do not have this situation under control whatsoever," The officer opened her mouth to retort however, this took place in a fleeting moment, and where it had disappeared, compromise arose.

"What have you got?"

"While I was airborne I scouted the entire ministry square. The Bolivians are working with this masked man and they have warfare grade weapons. That beats what you guys are carrying and that limits what I can fight back with, especially since there are bystanders in the area,"

"What are we going to do then? If we can't get past those blockades we cannot get the crowd to safety. I don't even know if they want to leave. They are there watching, like it's some sort of concert," she tutted.

"The man is playing on the bad reputation of the politicians. The whole thing is a gimmick, once I get in, the shows over," N.O.M.A. said with such confidence that anyone that didn't know better would think he either had a tactical plan already formed or an arsenal of mechanical measures at his suit's disposal. To the well informed, he had both.

"You just said yourself; we can't get in with the Bolivians there,"

"Don't worry about them. Call Boston's Base and request backup, tell them that you will sort out payment later. Once I've taken out the Bolivian blockade on the East road, don't engage until army backup arrives,"

"I never thought I'd hear the day that you'd tell us to call Boston's Base. Didn't you denounce them when the protests were going on?" said the police leader.

"Keep your friends close and your enemies closer," trailing his words, the metal at his arm's length retracted in place and two bladed, crimson arcs appeared by his back, in the shape of a X.

"Same applies to you guys too, by the way," his honesty was soon lost in the sounds of the suits hover technology and with another lost second, N.O.M.A.'s encounter with the police was just a memory.

Puoid – Quoid – Zuoid – like red thunder, a figure struck ground from skyward.

Puoid – Quoid – Zuoid – the sound of the suits systems acquiring targets.

Puoid – Quoid – Zuoid – Bolivian gun flashes met the walls of tungsten.

Puoid – Quoid – Zuoid – one by one, five crimson punches left them slumbered.

Puoid – Quoid – Zuoid – more feral hearted goons burst through the lorry that was blocking the east road toward the ministry square. With the crimson hero in their view, they all unloaded. Handgun bullets ricocheted from the surface, whereas the automatic rifle rounds that met their target, buried themselves within the tungsten. Even the exposed parts of his suit (his lower face and right hand) where shots would have otherwise struck, were instinctively covered without command. By the time their last rounds were fired, the suit rearranged its metals to their original places. The sum of their actions left the Bolivian men with one maxim; even if the man underneath the suit was an ordinary man, he was not wearing an ordinary suit.

"When your boss visits you in prison, let him know he picked the wrong guy to work with," N.O.M.A. slammed a palm to the floor before engaging his X shaped wings that propelled him tens of feet into the sky. Whilst the Crimson Angel was now far beyond their sight, he left a peculiar crimson orb in his place. The Bolivians argued amongst themselves what exactly it was, even descending into insults in their native language, however not one of them could have predicted what would come next. In half a blink, the crimson orb destructed, releasing a ten meter gush of red mist. The sounds of dropped guns could be heard and then, the sounds of collapsing bodies. Eleven seconds later the Crimson Angel rejoined the now red scene, but with a gas mask formed at his helmet. He would fare better. The Bolivians on the floor were conscious and grunting, however the gas had crippled them into complete immobility. N.O.M.A. emerged from the red storm, with a slightly blemished uniform and the concord of the Indiana street team, who could move closer to the crime scene for the first time that day.

"Don't get too close to the red stuff. It is action gas. Breath that in and you're paralysed for three hours at least," he warned.

"Where did you get that stuff from, they don't even give to our officers," said the unit leader.

"A little gift I got abroad. The Bolivians at the other blockades are going to rush here to help. The gas should take care most of them and I'm sure you can handle the rest,"

"Don't worry about us, we know what we can handle. We've never arrested so many people close to the Bolivian Conglomerate before; I'm hoping we can get more information on their leader,"

"Are you going to try and take me in after ma'am?" N.O.M.A.'s gas mask realigned itself to another part of the suit.

"Just get that masked bastard so we can end all of this," she told him. The Crimson Angel need not be prompted twice because his suit had powered into propulsion. The crimson suit was the parenthesis to his intentions and the extrinsic zenith to anything the human race had come remotely close to creating, technologically speaking.

Before, he knew it, Kai was a hundred feet in the sky; an average day for him, had he not been on duty. He arrowed toward the ministry building that dared to reach the heights he was currently, but fell short with its steep, but quadrangular roofing. As he glided toward the third floor balcony, he could see three figures become clearer and clearer. Two submissive captives and a hell-raiser for a captain. As he neared the ministry windows, the next few moments were introduced by N.O.M.A. diving into the room at full speed, but there were small and pivotal details in the scene that protracted the first encounter between N.O.M.A. and Midas. This deep seated analysis was conducted by the recording module in N.O.M.A.'s visor as the events were beyond the privy of those watching in real time. It all happened without the notice of a moment. As N.O.M.A. was mid dive, Midas had fired his revolver and given his targets velocity, this resulted in a point blank bullet to the suits shoulder, moreover, a noticeable change in N.O.M.A.'s dive path. Instead of tackling Midas, he rocketed toward the wall behind, but not before his suit could activate a series of mind boggling tasks. The impact side of his suit bloated just before impact, giving it the quality of a crash bag. From the forearm of his unbloated arm, a newly formed grappling hook shot outward, collected the leg of Midas and pulled him along for the ride. The chest of his suit detached itself and like a mouse trap, clamped itself to the masked man once the hook pulled him nearer. The efficiency of these feats could not be quantified by a human, as before Kai had even endured his crash landing and before Midas could even suspect such, the encounter was over. N.O.M.A. had already detained his target. Even without mouth ties, the on watching politicians would have nothing to say. They blinked blankly at the utter blinkerdom that was going on before them; not sure whether to be more confused by the crimson shape shifting suit or Midas' agendas.

"I was not expecting that... quite an entrance," pressured breaths could be heard behind Midas' mask, as he struggled to free himself from his crimson clasp. It did not budge at all; the previous tungsten chest plate had now assumed the form of a tight leather. As Midas continued to try and talk the leather into relaxation, Kai rose from his fall. He gripped his right shoulder as tight as his bony hands would allow. He had large portions of his suit missing, leaving his black, mesh under suit visible. Despite his lacking appearance, his objective was complete. He limped toward the captured Midas. He made his journey across the room shorter by making sure to reel him closer with the grappling hook still attached to his leg. When he stood over the masked man, the grappling line returned to a compartment on his suit, as did most of the leather clasp, as he made contact with it. All that remained were four slim metal restraints, which pinned Midas to the floor by his ankles and wrists.

"You both can relax now" N.O.M.A. informed the two politicians, who were still kneeling. He stopped inches from Midas' body, *"Who are you and why have you done this?"* came N.O.M.A.'s menacing equalizer.

"I think you know who I am by now; they must have said my name a hundred times on the way here,"

"I said," N.O.M.A. slammed one of his tungsten boots onto Midas' chest, *"Who are you and why have you done this?"*

"Why don't you take off the mask and find out Crims," Midas panted.

"I don't have to do anything right now. You see, I won. I won and I have all the time to get what I want until the cops and reinforcements turn up and take you away. You see, that's how it usually goes. I could take your mask of right now, but you are going to tell me because you don't want to know what I am capable of,"

"Well, you're not capable of a gripping monologue, you're putting me to sleep here – owch," Midas squirmed as N.O.M.A. applied more pressure on his chest.

*"It doesn't matter who is under your mask because you are
insignificant. The whole ministry gimmick was interesting
while it lasted, but I want to know about the Bolivian
Conglomerate that you somehow have got here, and you're going
to tell me everything,"* N.O.M.A. demanded.

"I threw this whole occasion for you and you don't want to see who is under the mask? Are you sure?"

*"The cops are going to run this building within the next ten
minutes, either you start talking or you are gonna get a one
way trip to hallows island,"*

"You really know how to get someone's attention, I bet you tell all the girls tha-
Owch!" more weight gave way from N.O.M.A.'s boot, as did the rest of Midas' air supply.

"Looks like they'll need ambulances as well as police then,"
N.O.M.A. decided. For the first time during their exchange, Midas was forcefully out of words; however the smile of the crass golden mask stayed. No matter how long Kai applied the pressure, the smile did not budge. A chill brushed his bones and shortly after, so did an electrocution.

ZZZZAAAPPP!!!

A numbing taser blast was pressed against his sternum; an area of his exposed undersuit. Kai watched as he fell to the floor in a clash of tungsten and discombobulating waves. He watched the information screen on his visor disappear as his suit assumed sleep mode, due to his paralysis. He could not believe his eyes when he was turned around to face the view above. Not only was a newly invigorated Midas standing over him, but he was now joined by the female politician that had been tied throughout the whole episode.

"Hey Crims," Midas, greeted him, "Some people call her Linzy, but I call her a decoy. Maybe you should pay more attention to 'insignificant faces'," Midas' irony was complete when he removed the crimson restraints from his wrist, which were now the equivalent of string due to his suits sleep mode. Kai tried with all his might to move, (the suit read muscle movement to turn online), but his efforts were useless in the face of his bodily shock. He now had to face the embarrassing about face caused by his arrogance, which Midas' was enjoying whole heartedly.

"It must be so painful to be where you are. Had the chance to take my mask off and sail away as the hero of today. But, now you're the one down there, you have no idea who I am and you're now probably more curious than ever. Do you know who doesn't take good advice when they're told? Children and politicians," Midas had a darkness about him when he divulged further.

"You see no matter what you tell a child or a politician they are going to say and do whatever they need to get that candy. Oh, that sweet-sweet money. They will even lie," he continued, "But now you are down there and I'm up here. I'm going to put a bullet through Mr What'shisface head and then I'm going to throw you from this building, so you can have a think about your great failure today before you die."

Midas picked up his golden revolver from the floor and rubbed it clean with the inside of his oversized blazer. As foretold, he aimed the weapon at the last politician who threw numerous proposals at him in attempt to deter his death.

BANG!

The proposals went up in the air along with his blood from the direct headshot. Even with new bloodstains, the mask kept its twenty-four carat smile. Screams could be heard from the crowds that were still gathered at the ministry steps, despite their lack of visibility in the scene above.

"Throw him off the building," Midas ordered the lady, "and then tell the Bolivians that I'm ready to be picked up," Kai hoped he could buy some time from the jesting ways that Midas' had shown so far, however he watched himself be dragged by his wounded shoulder in the cold silence that only murderers operate in. He heard every glass shard, every scrunched paper and every pool of blood on his journey toward the edge of the balcony. The moment when he realised that his hope to buy time would be unfulfilled, was the same moment he realised that Midas' had used the same tactic in order to allow his decoy enough time to free herself and attack him from behind. If arrogance had reduced him to one eye, so to speak, his complacency had refused him the ability to see clearly and even a suit like his could not compensate for that.

"I would say I don't care who is under your helmet, but I already know," said Midas. Kai found himself breathless when the security of solid ground left him, and the autumn winds could be felt trying to catch his fall. The Indiana city police, the Bolivian escape men and the national television reporters were all witness as a defeated N.O.M.A. fell from the third floor of the ministry building toward the crowd of innocent spectators at the steps. The crowd lost density as many tried to escape from the tungsten projectile falling from directly above them. From within the fleeting crowd a crimson light coruscated...

CHAPTER 5

The Crimson Tent

Ministry Square

Heavens Conquest, Indiana

NORU LOGS – Present Day

Unknown user: Oh my god! Noru, is he ok?! Is he alive?!

NORU: *I engaged the parachute module. The fall should not have been fatal from that height; however he has likely incurred some injuries. Unfortunately, I cannot access my medical modules so I cannot assess the extent of any damage until the systems are back online.*

Unknown user: What happened up there, how comes his suit turned into this –

tent?

NORU: *I could not get a visual reading through the material of your shoulder carrier you had trapped me in. When the N.O.M.A. suit is out of operation, I am programmed to send a specific frequency of which the suit deploys an emergency stabilisation field - The Crimson Tent.*

Unknown user: Oh my god, he fell from so high.

NORU: *Yes a height that would have resulted in instant death. The reason why I have been programmed with emergency modules.*

Unknown user: What is this Crimson Tent supposed to do?

NORU: *The Crimson Tent module serves three purposes. The first is to protect the suit until it resynchronises with the operational core - which will bring the informational modules back online. The second purpose is to send a low frequency distress signal to our live satellite. The third purpose is for it to mimic a pojangmacha.*

Unknown user: I did not understand what that last one was at all.

NORU: *The pojangmacha is a traditional street stall tent that is prominent in the region of South Korea. This third purpose does not better system or satellite functionality, but I am lead to think it contributes to Mr. Boston's mental health.*

Unknown user: Ok, ok enough about that! We need medical supplies.. a first aid... anything... why is there not anything here?!

NORU: (Processing) this is not an oversight. When the suit is synchronised to the operational core I can replicate information such as this first aid you speak of.

Unknown user: Replicate information?

NORU: Yes, if the suit has enough physical capacity, it can replicate most types of physical information.

Unknown user: How is that possible?

Kai Boston: Enough Noru. End transmission.

END OF TRANSMISSION

Despite his entire body ringing with pain, Kai pulled himself upward until he was seated on two elbows. There was no real cushion for a forty foot fall, not even the adaptable features on his N.O.M.A. suit. He felt heavy headed and he discerned his surroundings with heavier eyes. From right to left he could see the sloped ceilings meet at a triangular center. These were ceilings he had not seen since trying the protocol for the first time during its inception. His exemplary track record whilst wearing the suit had not given reason for the Crimson Tent to be deployed, but there was a first time for everything. Including the situation before him, which would never have crossed his suspicion until a perfectly symmetrical line of birth marks came into his view.

"Are you ok?" asked Damia Ascot. Kai tried to muster words, but given the depth of his confusion, they sank before they left his mouth. Damia proceeded to scratch the side of her wide forehead, perhaps in embarrassment.

"What the f*ck are you doing in my tent, Damia?" finally, Kai burst out.

"I'm seeing if you were alive, moron!"

"That doesn't exactly answer my question," Kai sat upwards further, to an aching seat, "besides, I do not need anyone looking out for me."

"Really? If I did not happen to have Noru on me, you probably would have been dead," she countered.

"I can confirm that without my emergency signal, a fall from twenty feet or more inside the suit, would

have resulted in an instant fatality," Noru confirmed. Kai seized the circular, crimson node from Damia's side of the tent.

"Noru, not now. Not in front of her anyway," he then released the node to hover as it always did.

"Exactly," Damia stood to her feet with a forceful exhalation, "now how do you make this thing open. I want to get out of here,"

"We can't leave," Kai said.

"What do you mean can't? Why?"

"The suit is in emergency recovery mode. We cannot exit this tent until the systems have resynchronised and are back online."

"So we physically can't leave?"

"Nope. No one can get in either; the tent is made from tungsten. No one's getting in or out unless you are a tank or something."

"Your suit turned into a tent, how is that even possible, Kai?" asked Damia.

"Why do you assume it began as a suit in the first place?" Kai could see the clockwork of her logic reverse in real time. She stared into thin air for a few seconds, before taking a pensive seat opposite him. Kai continued to watch her as he massaged his aching forearms with his bony hands. Between the fact that she had shown a strong dislike for him when Tre Moon first introduced them, to the fact that she had taken it upon herself to remove the Noru node from its observatory (behind his back), he was also seeking answers. The tent was hollow but it was also sturdy; there was no escaping the forthcoming inquest. It was only Kai Boston and Damia Ascot now.

"Why did you take Noru from the bunker? We are supposed to be monitoring the Spectre, what if he escapes?" the last thing Kai wanted, was for Tre's efforts to be undone within his jurisdiction.

"The Spectre has been asleep since the day we placed him in there. You were right, without consuming light, it is weak,"

"But still, why take Noru?"

"I took Noru because I wanted to find out more about you," Damia exclaimed. After this admission, her eyelids fluttered over her ovular eyes, but she held contact with Kai's slanted ones.

"Why didn't you just ask me yourself?" he said.

"Because I don't know if I can trust you, I don't know if Tre can either," she told him. Kai gave a hearty laugh that lasted twenty seconds, the echoes from the hollow tent made it seem twice as long.

"You, can't trust, me? This city needs me!"

"Not today it didn't. Those politicians deserved to be exposed, they are criminals themselves," Damia said.

"You were supporting the man in the golden mask?"

"I don't know. I just think it was just. He made them face all of the horrible things that they have been doing in their position."

"Well Damia, fortunately you don't get to decide. That mad man murdered someone. I'm going to bring him in as soon as we get out of here," Kai's voice echoed confidently.

"Judging by what happened earlier, you may need Tre's help,"

"Tre's help? For what, this is just a man in a mask,"

"I think we both know that he is more than just a man in a mask. You saw how many Bulgarian men he had. The leader of the Bulgarian Conglomerate does not just work with anybody," Damia progressively leant forward hoping to see reason in the young Commander, however, all she came to realise was that the crimson tent was modeled after his pride.

"I'll handle it myself," he said, "I don't need anyone to tell me what I'm dealing with. The Bulgarians have supplied him with firepower that's for sure, he was even using a military grade taser. Nothing else can put my suit offline like that. Next time he won't get close enough," Kai believed that calling for Specular's help was like dousing a dying flame with a waterfall. Unnecessary and ultimately, pointless. For him, bringing the man in the golden mask to law was easy, however deciphering the criminal relationships he had made, and knowing what possible arsenal he will have at his disposal upon their next encounter, was a task that could only be handled by himself and the consummate knowledge that his field in intelligence had given him. The margin between preparation and execution was extremely fine, and preparation was something that Tre's superpowers could not solve.

"You can't do it can you," Damia head was upon the patronising orbit of a shake, "You can't even bring yourself to ask for his help?"

"Trust me, when I need help I'll get it. I don't need help with this," Kai said.

"We can't do everything alone, I thought you of all people would know that," she said. Kai pivoted on his seat, so much as to break eye contact.

"Noru, how long left?"

"Systems are still down, so I cannot say exactly. I predict five more hours."

"Five more hours?!" Damia and Kai rhymed.

"I don't know if I can stay in this thing for that long, is there even ventilation?" Damia clambered toward one of the sloped ceilings.

"I can assure you there is a sophisticated and functioning ventilation system. This is an emergency space, not a torture chamber."

"Could have fooled me…"

"We may need to review the Crimson Tent's design once systems are back online Noru," Kai announced.

```
"The design was pre-approved and re-approved by
yourself, Mr. Boston."
```

"I know, but maybe we should add an eject feature for people who sneak in," when he looked at his guest from the corner of his eye, he was given a scorching look in return. With only their heated relationship occupying the space, the tent began to resemble something more of a stove. Shortly after, Kai shed the top layer of his black under suit. It was the sight of his bruised shoulder that evoked the first act of warmth.

"That looks pretty bad," Damia stepped toward Kai slowly. Her eyebrow curled further upward when she saw exactly how far the purple patch spread across his right arm; from his pectoral to the top of his shoulder. Kai glanced at his shoulder, chuckled in a priapic way – say; the purple bruise was as faint as the echoes in the room and assumed a modest groove, which was a ruse for his usual hubris.

"I'm not going to lie, it hurts like Sh!t – AGH, what are you doing?!" halfway through his words, Damia took it upon herself to place a hand directly to the sore.

"There's no medical supplies in here," she began applying slight pressure to the purple site, "if we are going to be in here for this long, it will need something."

"What on earth is that supposed to do?" Kai found himself inhaling sharply.

"I used to live on a farm back in Dallas. Some time ago. I used to sneak out to ride the horses from the stable at night because my mother said I wasn't responsible enough. Guess she was right – horse riding and dark fields are not the best combination. I used to get all types of bruises from my falls, so you kind of learn how to deal with them. Either that or get grounded right?" Damia continued with the therapy and though he did not know whether it would heal the wound any faster, he settled.

"Didn't take you for a country type of person. You seem to know your way around the city," said Kai.

"I've learnt. You kind of have to here, so much stuff crazy stuff going on these days."

"As soon as we get out of here, I'm going to catch him by the way," Kai reminded her at a half turn.

"Alright – alright, big shot. What I meant earlier is that I can help. I helped Tre figure out his powers, plus I know this city very well. There are only so many places Midas can hide," she said.

"I don't know if you noticed, but I'm not Tre. I didn't just put on a suit to settle some personal scores, I've been doing this for a long time – without help- AGH, watch it man!" his rebuttal was met with a particularly firm rub of the affected area.

"Sorry," came a toneless apology, "it doesn't matter why Tre became Specular, at least I know that he is a good person. No one knows why you do what you do; no one even knows what N.O.M.A. really stands for."

Pride was another layer of armour and though it was not to be physically reckoned, arbitrary accusations, misrepresentation and an accumulation of censure was ensured to set a defensive individual such as Kai on an unlikely venture. Damia already knew his secret identity, today he would take her down the road of his life. From his cocoon days in Korea to his days of flight in Indiana, the butterfly effect had taken his life to heights he did not previously think possible. But, like all butterflies, he started a vulnerable larva. He set his slanted eyes on Noru.

"Noru, what have you got for me."

"I have pre-recorded your favourite LOGS on my node, for times of boredom Mr. Boston, would you like me to play one?"

"Our guest is curious about me, how I even got the suit. Let's show her,"

"Are you sure Mr. Boston, this LOG has been locked by yourse-"

"Authorised! Play the recording," the usual tone of confidence in his voice had parted.

NORU LOGS – Piki Village, South Korea - 1989

Noru Ohama: Hello, hello. I hope this thing is recording. I, I am making this video for my unborn child. I don't know whether you will be a boy, or a girl but I know you will be beautiful. A true, Ohama. I wish I did not have to make this video, but things are getting worse in this territory, the United States army are gaining more and more control every day. They are controlling our trade and even where we can and cannot go. We should have foreseen what allowing them to set up a defense outpost in our village meant. The soldiers do whatever they want, I mean anything. They are dogs. Our village is not safe anymore. And I fear neither are you. Once they find out you are like them, (whimpers) they may try to get rid of you, to cover up what they are doing here. What they have done to me. I am expecting you soon my beautiful child, but you cannot grow up here, you mustn't. It is this – thing – that has drawn the soldiers here. They have seen what we have built and the see us as a threat. This Basta Matrix, this crimson artifact. It is more powerful than we ever thought. It can hold more information than any library and it can replicate anything we place upon it. The Americans have not discovered how we have built the things we have, but it is only a matter of time. The Basta Matrix is a tool of war, and whatever you do, please do not live the kind of life we have. Using a tool, a power that we have no concern using. If the rest of the world discover what the Basta Matrix can do, it could incite a third world war. We have endured terrible things to keep this secret, to bury it away. I have endured unspeakable things, thinking that the Matrix could let us live in peace once again. But it would be a short lived peace. True power is not meant to be controlled by us humans, I realise that now. I pray every day that you will live through this – our mistakes. I love you, my angel.

END OF TRANSMISSION

By the end of the sequence, Damia was set. The echoes of Noru Ohama's voice stayed with them long after. It was after this segment that it became clear that the voice of the Noru node, was modelled after the voice they had just heard.

"I'm sorry," Damia mouthed, "you didn't have to show me that."

"The American soldiers slaughtered most of my village when I was five years of age. The reason; an upcoming terrorist state, with destructive technology. But, they never found the matrix because it was given to me. Against my murdered mothers wishes. I never knew why they sent me away from the village until I learnt how to access the Matrix's information. It stores everything,"

"You didn't have to show me that,"

"Yeah I didn't. I could've listened to my Mother and never used the Basta Matrix too, but I will not stand by and watch more injustice go on when it can be prevented. My Mother was wrong." Kai buried his face into his purpled shoulder. Beneath the armour and the arrogance was a bruised soul. Damia crawled to a seat beside him and the Crimson Tent held echoes of pain. Echoes the rest of the world would not see.

CHAPTER 6

Dojo Life (The Midas Effect)

The public hostage scene at Indiana's ministry buildings shook the continent of America. Even more shook, was the city of Heavens Conquest and with his conquest now at large, it was Midas and his golden mask that was scarred into the people's hearts. The city was shaken without tectonics, just histrionics and a golden revolver. Not knowing who Midas would take aim at next, the city became extremely fretful and the emergence of the Bolivian Conglomerate from the shadows only enforced this feeling further. The fact that the Bolivian men were able to secure Midas from the scene of the crime and return him to the unknown depths of Indiana's criminal underworld, was evidence of their dominion of the state. Police efforts were but hiccough's to their livelihood and given how equipped they were proving to be, even forces such as the SWAT team were but a swat in the air to them; a nuisance at best. Their army approved armoury made sure of that. The month of August 2012 also marked the rise of a social stir, dubbed the 'Midas Effect'. Many members of the public became convinced that they sighted or knew personally, persons who matched Midas' universal description which was: around six foot tall, Caucasian, a bald head and a lanky posture. The Midas Effect permeated in Heavens Conquest, as did distrust. Traitors, false accusations and public displays of mania were the first tremors of the Midas Effect. Those who thought they knew who Midas was, were proven to be mistaken and those who knew that they did not know, were closest to knowing anything. The Midas Effect twisted fact and inference so well, that the weight of the IDP's (Indiana Police Department) suspect gathering was based on nothing but guesswork. Workaholic interrogators were given overtime, as time after time, their given suspects failed to bring them any closer to finding out who the man in the golden mask really was. Thus, despite only one public appearance, Midas became somewhat of an enigma. He had the authorities in more of a knot than *Magnolia*. He had the people pacified in the palm of his hand and the Bolivians on call with so much as the roll of his shoulder. The Midas Effect – it became a phrase, where the mention of his name would cause a head turning, Jimmy Turner spurred, turn of events, where a neighbour was perceived to be as trustworthy as a hand in the mouth of an alligator. Allegations reigned true, because no one knew, who knew who. Trust was as thin as the line between Tre and Blue Moon and not even the rule of the late Submirenean, King Mitus, could unite the differences. The Midas Effect. Never in Indiana's history had forensic scientists pried so hard to identify a man. After all, Midas was just a mortal in a golden mask, but he was also well researched. His brown, stitched, leather gloves ensured that his areas of contact were as indistinguishable as his face. Without their ace in the hole, ACE-V fingerprint analysis techniques, even the forensic route failed. The race to uncover Midas' identity reached an uncomfortable plane. The Midas Effect would remain.

NORU LOGS – Present Day

NORU: *Good morning, Mr. Boston. I want to remind you that you have ignored all three routine alarms to get up for work at the army base. I am afraid that you are now projected to be an hour and thirty seven minutes late to start.*

Kai Boston: Tell me something I don't know.

NORU: *(Processing) Gustave Le Bon was a leading researcher of crowd psychology, in his essay 'The crowd: A Study of the Popular Mind' he wrote: "In a crowd every sentiment and act is contagious, and contagious to such a degree that an individual readily sacrifices his personal interest to the collective interest.*

Kai Boston: I didn't mean it like that, enough facts, Noru.

NORU: *Understood. Perhaps you should let me process an implied discourse module.*

Kai Boston: There isn't a module for that kind of thing. You can disable all future alarms, I won't be going into work for a while.

NORU: *I think I should remind you, as per the Base's protocol: Sergeant Boston does not take unexplained absence well with senior members of staff.*

Kai Boston: Trust me there's a reason... I want to run a few things by you.

NORU: *Please continue, Mr. Boston.*

Kai Boston: The first thing is the Crimson Tent. Is there anything you can do to make the switch back to the suit less visible? The more people can see of the suit, the more weaknesses we will have.

NORU: *I can detonate the action gas module that we obtained from the island of Guyana. This will mask the tent as it transforms back into the suit.*

Kai Boston: And risk paralysing everyone nearby... hm. Harsh. Cancel request.

NORU: *Request cancelled.*

Kai Boston: Also, I want you to open every past video LOG and run specifications for anyone who matches the following description: six foot or above in height, bald, Caucasian and skinny.

NORU: *I have run the following specification 'Six foot or above in height - bald hairstyle, Caucasian ethnicity - ectomorph body type' on the visors combined footage. I have returned more than one hundred results and counting.*

Kai Boston: Run layering and try a person who matches Midas' dimensions.

NORU: *The visor did not capture sufficient footage before going offline, to form Midas' dimensions*

Kai Boston: F*ck! There's gotta be another way to find out who this jackass is.

NORU: *Mr. Boston, there is currently a perception called the Midas Effect - where multiple people are reporting to have seen Midas. It may stem from a mix of fear and familiarity after the event. It seems even you are directing your attention to the details of this description. Given that this man wears a mask to hide his identity, we can also gather that he would take other measures to hide other features that would make him recognizable, like height and body shape.*

Kai Boston: You cannot hide things like that, Noru.

NORU: *Midas is not the average person. The Midas Effect may seem logical but that doe not mean it will lead us to finding him. The description you have given may be intentionally misleading.*

Kai Boston: He is average and you know why? He makes mistakes too; he should not have mentioned that he knows who I am.

NORU: *No record on file. I assume the suit was offline when this was said?*

Kai Boston: Yes. Run the specifications on people I know personally.

NORU: *Mr. Boston, I repeat, the Midas Effect is rife and it may-*

Kai Boston: I don't care, run it!

NORU: *(Processing) One match returned - Master Dommi Mattias: owner of 'Dojo Life' gym in downtown faith, Heavens Conquest.*

Kai Boston: Master Mattias huh? Finally got my reason to shut his lecturing ass up.

NORU: *On a side note - your monthly membership to the Dojo expires this week. Would you like me to renew?*

Kai Boston: Don't bother.

END OF TRANSMISSION

Dojo Life Gym

Downtown, Faith Borough (West), Heavens Conquest

Dojo Life was a small time gym with a big heart. The same sentiment it taught to its students, which ranged from juniors who were dabbling into the martial arts for the first time, to nationally competitive fighters who came to harden their fists. Located in the downtown area of the Faith borough, the attendees lacked anything but this. Master Dommi Mattias, (an eastern European bred, practicing veteran of a whopping eleven martial arts) attended keenly to every single person who entered his gym. He would first learn of their name, then of their motivation, as in his own words; understanding intentions could better the intention in one's strike. Like pikes in the water, many amateurs would disrupt the flow of collective classroom sessions, but Master Mattias never let the river of students continue with someone left behind. Be like water, was the likeminded inspiration behind training and like the late and great Bruce Lee, the dojo was no stranger to dedication. It contained: full body punching bags full of sand, enough overhead punching pads to make a rhythm from your hands. Buick yip wooden dummies and a wall stand with a selection of Bo staffs of various lengths. Across the room were extravagant wing chun mannequins, excruciating conditioning ropes, pilates pine-pillars, karate style nunchukus and for the most ambitious, a sparring circle in the centre of the room. The sparring circle was the shape and colour of the traditional, oriental rising sun, and the rest of the dojo simmered the shade of a soaring orange. All considerable tournaments and contests were conducted in the sparring circle and the entire dojo would often watch when this did happen. The crowd would act like water, forming around the circle only to come crashing inwards once a spar had respectfully ended. The dojo culture was strong and as far as Kai's deduction had taken him, so was the owners association to a certain criminal he was looking for. Kai Boston entered the dojo on that same midweek afternoon. His white gi was fitted around his frame and tightened at the waist by a crimson belt. Not a single word of greet came from the young commander upon enter, he just surveyed the dojo for his target and he found results rather quickly. Master Mattias was located toward the left of the room and was guiding the shoulders of a member of the dojo that looked around Kai's age (twenty-three). He stepped directly toward the Master until a junior member of the gym placed himself in his path. Kai's slit eyebrows jolted upward like a crossbow upon release.

"Hey man, how comes you always wear the red belt, aren't you ever gonna rank up?" came the boy's light voice.

"You think you're funny?" Entertained by the boy's suggestion, Kai stopped mid-walk. Sharp canines could be seen at the side of his mouth when he let out a simper of retaliation, "if you had a belt like this you would wear it all the time too."

"Nah, I wouldn't stop at red. I want to be a black belt."

"Oh so you think it's the belt that makes you good, so how about this," Kai crouched some until the boy could hear his lowered voice, "what if I beat Master Mattias in a contest? What would you think about belts then?"

"Pfttt," the young boy chucked his head backward in disbelief, "you can't beat Master Mattias. He has had that black belt for years."

"You got dice for those words?" Kai was willing to double over his words with results and when it came to immodest, inner city idioms, he was willing to throw them out with leisure. In the proverbial betting grounds of combat, he was going to roll sixes every time, he that was that sure of his abilities.

"Master has taught a lot people how to defend themselves, even if you did beat him, it wouldn't make him any less of a Master. Everyone loses sometimes." For this, Kai did not have an immediate response. These words affected him more than he wanted. The benefits of a defeat. The virtue of submission. There were none. His home village had surrendered to stronger powers and he lost his mother, family and culture because of it. They were too weak to defend themselves. Too weak to consider anything but submission. Having come from the splinters of his destroyed village, he had to build a stronger future. Defeat was not an option in a city plagued in paroxysm, especially when carrying the shame of the name Boston. He was born defeated but he would die before being conquered again. By the time he stood again, his smile had lost its concavity.

"When you have something to protect, you'll learn that there is no room to lose. Might be the last thing you do," said Kai.

"Don't let this asshole pick on you." Came a new voice behind him. Kai could have sworn that the insult was genuinely unprovoked, until Helle Bushida came into their view, also wearing a white gi (in a tighter fit), a blue belt and arms crossed so tightly into each other, a neutral onlooker could swear Kai was unauthorized to be on the premises.

"I'm surprised you made it here," Kai shimmied backward as Helle raised a fist in reply.

"When we get out of here, I am going to kill you, Kai," Helle said through a white mouth guard, which gave her the appearance of a particularly feral, hazelnut poodle.

"If you get the chance. He is going to challenge Master Matt-"

"Junior class is over, why don't you wait outside?" Helle spoke over the boy intentionally. After the boy had walked away disappointed that he would not see the upcoming contest, Helle grabbed a handful of Kai's gi gear and pulled him to a quiet side of the dojo. She was clearly enlivened by her physical workouts up until that point, because during their exchange, she hopped and bent on the spot as if Kai was a body bag himself.

"Challenging Master Mattias, are they feeding you ok at the army?!"

"I don't expect you to understand and I didn't ask you to either,"

"As your friend I want to understand especially before you go and embarrass yourself,"

"This is exactly why I wasn't going to tell you, if only that kid would shut his damn–"

"Challenging the Master will not get you a black belt!"

"Does it look like I want a black belt?"

"What do you want then?!"

"To prove something to myself," Kai then stepped around Helle and though she looked ready to shout in hot appeal, she spoke a soft tune instead,

"Be careful, please..."

Things like advice and sympathy rarely passed Kai's self-assured air, and Helle's words were no different. In his world, arrogance and the sky were the same thing. Without it, he could not reach the heights he had since coming to America. He was almost certain that Master Mattias was the man he had encountered at the ministry buildings recently, the evidence did not line up any other way. If this was indeed the truth and both men knew who each other truly were, today would be a contest of character. No masks, no weapons, just skill.

"Master Mattias, I challenge you to a contest. No restrictions." Kai called finally. As the sound left his mouth, he could not help the wave of uncertainty that swept him. The temples on the side of his head crumbled inward as he clenched his jaw. Sweat developed at the back of his head and dived. The destination; his neck that now resembled a long grain farm, because when Master Mattias responded, its hairs immediately stood on end.

"I accept your challenge, Kai Boston,"

The entire dojo joined the outskirts of the rising sun, sparring circle. So many on watchers were shoulder to shoulder that, combined, their gi's made a curtain of white. Attentions were not restricted to inside the dojo, because passerby's who happened to look inside, stopped to witness the spectacle. Both martial artists were positioned inside the rising sun circle. Master Mattias, (who was Caucasian, had a bald hairstyle and stood at roughly six foot two in height) faced both of his palms toward each other and kept his humble pose, all the while, Kai taped his wrists and powdered his knuckles. The start of the contest came when both men naturally ceased their pre-fight routines and made eye contact. Master Mattias bent by the waist, as showing deference was a common act in the arts and in return, Kai wiped at his nose with a single finger – just to test the waters. With one ungracious gesture, a storm began in the crowd. His indifference caused odium and ordain, especially amongst the senior members of the dojo.

The competitors themselves began to form their own guises of water; Master Mattias swayed from side to side, both of his arms were raised, but limp. In other words, the archetype of the drunken monkey fighting style. Kai embodied the sundry state of water; he would invert his facing position every so often and when he did, so would his martial stance. At any given switch, one could expect: Taekwondo, Hapkido or Tang-Soo-Do. He dubbed this transitional fighting style, 'Korea's Lottery' and aside from the questionable methods Tre Moon had used during their duel at Boston's Base, Kai was undefeated when it came to hand to hand combat.

"Let's go," Kai thought, and with his first advance forward, the contest began. The spar started with numerous sidesteps as both men tried to get an attacking angle. Finer footwork could not be found at a Cecchetti method rehearsal and when Master Mattias dipped forward for the first strike, it was one of purpose. A wild arm cropped the tip of Kai's combed fringe, but no longer than three seconds later, the same arm had come full circle for another attempt, which knocked the young man directly in the neck. The crowd jumped in volume as a flurry of strikes and blocks followed. The strikes were conducted at such speeds that Kai flinched moments after he had already blocked them. Each of Kai's attacks proved as hard as targeting an actual drunken monkey, Mattias was agile and unpredictable.

SMOK!

Separation came when the full brunt of the Master's knee caught the side of Kai's face. Proving to be as lethal as it sounded, Kai fell to one knee.

"You have reached your ceiling. As long as you remain arrogant, you have nothing else to attain," said Master Mattias.

"You of all people," Kai raised his head, revealing a blackened eye, "should know how high I can go!" When he inverted his facing position, he assumed a Hapkido stance. The second clash between the fighters was on the terms that Kai preferred, brash and aggressive. Both men took hard hits, but the substantial counter based move set of Hapkido allowed Kai to capture one of Mattias' arms. With an entire limb in his grasp, Kai performed a hardened shoulder lock that brought the dojo's owner to his knees.

"Tell me!" Kai grimaced as he kept the Master's writhing arm in the lock.

"What, ARGH!"

"Just say it, just say who you are," he steadily forced the arm to the very edge of its natural edge of movement. At this point, Mattias was tapping the mat with his free hand.

"Ay, asshole, contest is over let him go,"

"I can't believe he beat Mattias..."

"You win, fights over Kai!"

The crowd was nervous and edged into the sparring circle ever so slightly. Many had the mind to physically separate the submission, but every single person in the dojo could see compulsion written on Kai Boston's face. He was clearly acting under some pretenses that had originated outside of the modest dojo.

"TELL US WHO YOU ARE!" Kai bellowed with such mania that for a split second, his taught face resembled an oni. It was this same moment that Helle, who had become distressed by the scenes, left the dojo at a run.

"Kai let him go. Whoever you think he is, he's not him," a member of the dojo bravely stepped forward and eased Kai's pressure on Master Mattias' arm. The presence of an innocent removed the red from his vision. Severance from the heat of combat made him realise that he had made a terrible misjudgment. Once again, the Midas Effect proved to be a vector and even the crimson heart of N.O.M.A. or the hard head of Kai Boston could not escape the pressures. Kai released Master Mattias' arm that had a flimsy aspect to it now that it was dislocated from its shoulder socket. Kai made a mask with his hands and the rest of the dojo put as much bodies between Kai and their beloved Master as possible.

"Don't come back here," said a senior member. Even through victory, he felt defeated and this was a new feeling. To everyone's surprise, Kai took the advice without a word of retaliation, he just grabbed his jacket and for the second time in his life, left a place he called home. Never to return again.

Kai exited the dojo and stood directly outside of it, as he attempted to clear his mind.

"I would say I don't care who is under your helmet, but that would be a lie. Because I already know you so well,"

Midas' words were implanted in his mind, and like the very best mind games, they made a man equipped with some of the best intelligence technology in the country, feel blind. Like the very best mind games, they would become louder at night. Like the very best mind games, it had made someone who measured themselves to the high standard of virtue, step out of line. Kai took this in his literal stride and though he had endured a small stagger from his fight, this was nothing compared to the figurative dagger in his side. If Master Mattias was not Midas, who was?

"So you are just going to leave without saying goodbye?" Helle stepped from the wall beside the dojo. In the fury of his thoughts, he had completely missed her. A lit cigarette sat between her right hand and there was a lump in her long neck from sobbing, hoarseness or perhaps both. Kai had drowned out all distractions when he tried to force admission from the Master.

"Please Helle, not now."

"If not now, then when. Am I even going to even see you again?"

"I can't come back here anymore."

"What is going on with you?" she whispered. The answer could have been as easy as untying his crimson belt and allowing her to see its morphing properties, but in truth, even this would not reveal the colour of his conscience currently, which was his newest battle.

"I'm not coming back here, Helle. I don't deserve to after that."

"You are right, you made a mistake and maybe you don't deserve it, but what about what you want?"

"What do I want?" he knew exactly what he wanted, a certain criminal captured. There was no way Helle could know that and so his expression darkened from confusion to investigation.

"Someone who understands you, the real you." After these words, the moment grew gradually imposing. Led by his slit eyebrows, his expression lightened from investigation to something more invitational. Helle's cheeks were now a blossom garden and the imposing moment even gained gravity, as it pulled them closer.

"Would you like to be my guest at the Avali award ceremony next month?" he asked, and then he watched as her face lit up like the city of Avali, Italy itself.

"It's a date." Said Helle.

CHAPTER 7

The Venia Strip

SERGEANTS OFFICE,

BOSTON'S BASE, HEAVENS CONQUEST

"Take a seat boy. Lieutenant Rashford, tell him why we are here today?"

"Certainly, it has come to our attention that the performance of the intelligence sector has fallen and it is in no doubt due to your lack of attendance recently, Mr. Boston."

"Continue,"

"Over the past two weeks you have only attended one of your scheduled ten shifts. Due to lack of warning, two armoury crates your team were supposed to trace are now lost somewhere in the Caribbean and without investigation into how many soldiers we needed to send, U.S. immigration have withdrawn their request for assistance at the Mexican border. One of our monthly sources of income,"

"Woops."

"This is not a goddamn game-"

"Sergeant, you made me Lieutenant of your army and trust me when I say I am just as unsettled as you are. You can have your piece with your son once I am finished."

"...go on,"

"Master Boston, no matter how significant you have been since being appointed head of intelligence and operations, without reasons for your lack of commitment, I'm afraid there may be ramifications for your recent actions,"

"Statement fourteen on the employee's contract: any damages, libel or lost earnings will not be at the expense of the individual, but will be absorbed by the faction," with his eyes closed, Kai continued to read from his mental notepad, "so what are these ramifications?"

"Master Boston, you better think very carefully before you speak. Your job may be on the line,"

"It is on the line everyday Lieutenant, even up in the control room." If a single raised leg on his chair was not indicative enough of his boredom, Kai leant his head against his knuckles in such a way that there could be no doubt. Lieutenant Rashford even with all the badges of service pinned to his chest, could not pinpoint exactly why such a young, promising prospect would get themselves into such a position. Sergeant Boston leant forward.

"Why are you doing this to your fathers base?"

"I know exactly why," his father's words came with a reddened complexion and frothing balls of spit, "he cannot stand to see my army doing well. This good for nothing will do anything to see me fail."

"Your army is destined to fail. I told you when I first joined. You won't get away with what you did to my mother or my village. I still mean that. Doesn't mean I won't work here just to see it burn though," Kai watched his father's square jaw grind with every passing sentence.

"I told you not to bring up Noru. You were young, you don't know what happened," warned the Sergeant.

"I know exactly what happened," Kai began, "you raped her and you took everything my village had worked for. You destroyed everything to cover your tracks and claimed glory back here in America. One day you will lose all of the blood money you have made and pay for every single person you have wronged."

"If I wanted to cover my tracks why did I take you in?" the meeting had descended into something much more personal and with the new wave of silence, the Sergeants latest questioned quaked Kai's mind. In the court of logic, this question did not hold up. Even if he was to scour the depths of the Basta Matrix, he was surely not to find the answer. Only the man he had the displeasure of calling his father truly knew. If a neutral onlooker was to look at history fiscally; the past had cost both Boston's the experience of a true father and son relationship. Lieutenant Rashford cleared his throat rather loudly to get a hold of the conversation, just like how his balding ponytail clambered to his freckled head by its few remaining hairs.

"Master Boston, it is clear you have some personal issues going on at the moment and while I do mean it when I say I hope you sort them out, you know better than anyone that we rank based on performance. I am afraid that you have been demoted as head of operational intelligence."

"Exc-f*&%-ing-use me?" Kai's thin eyes had become unusually wide.

"You have been demoted as head of intelligence," the elderly Lieutenant said calmly, "you will now report to your new boss. You can come in now." At Rashford's beckon, the door to the office opened, and through it stepped Liam Laverton – the recruit Kai had inducted no less than a three weeks ago.

"You got to be f*%$ing kidding me?" Kai looked over to his father, perhaps expecting an overrule, but Sergeant Boston had already placed a decided fist upon his own lips.

"Thank you once again, Sergeant" Liam Laverton (who was still wearing the same over gelled hairstyle) limped across the room to give the Sergeant a handshake. It was only on this occasion that Kai noted how meek the new recruit was built; he was slightly hunched and walked slowly as if he suffered from a bad back. Even his handshake had no tenacity to it. What hurt more than being dethroned, was that he had been dethroned by this type of a man.

"Sorry kid, nothing personal. Like I told you before, things have got to change. Guess now is the time," Laverton reached a hand to Kai's shoulder as if to soften the loss, however, Kai slapped it away with quickness. Pity was like a pitfall trap and he would not fall to the new standards.

"If you are seriously going to appoint a newbie as head of one of your sectors then I don't know what to say,"

"Mr. Laverton's contributions have been nothing but outstanding. He managed to extract some information from the detained men from our operation in Guyana. He is overseeing the detainment unit now. Laverton even coordinated the recent situation at the ministry buildings with the Indiana Police," said Rashford.

"Co-ordinated what? Our army didn't even come," Kai argued.

"You were not responsive or at base, so I made the call. The situation was too severe for us to get involved. We would have just wasted money travelling there and back," Laverton scratched his head.

"It's not about money! We are supposed to be providing a service to the people in our city; we are supposed to be restoring calm when there is disorder!" Kai rose from his seat, "besides, you guys trust this man? He has only been here for just under a month. Haven't even scratched the surface of what it takes to lead the army's operations sector."

"I trust this newbie as much as I trust you Kai," Sergeant Boston entered the crossfire, "in fact, I probably trust him more because I know that he won't shoot me in the back one day. And we both know you are just waiting for the day to take me down, boy." He pulled a thick cigar from his pocket and held it between his square teeth.

"I quit then," Kai undressed himself of his camouflage coat and then left it to find the floor. Liam looked more nervous than usual; as if he was on the brink of relinquishing his title just for the sake of calm. Sergeant Boston sniffed at this.

"If you leave the army you will no longer be entitled to the perks. Including the Boston pension scheme rates, free lease of land vehicles, free accommodation at the base and twenty-four-hour access to the control room," Lieutenant Rashford tried to put things into perspective for him but Kai had already weighed up the consequences. Not only would he be, by definition, homeless, but he would no longer have the tools that allowed him to watch over the city as N.O.M.A. Kai wore his pride like a hide and subsequently, his reply was thick skinned,

"Your loss." Kai snatched the control room key from around his neck and thew it to the table. He then reached for his crimson backpack by his chair and settled it on his back. The members in the room that were expecting reconsideration or negotiation on his part were destined to be left waiting. He left the room double the man, but only half the hero. Without the control room to update the links between his satellite, camera feeds and suit, his operation had little direction. He paced down the long hallways of the base for perhaps, the last time. Whilst he considered whether to first rent a hotel or establish a new satellite hotspot, a crimson node formed from his backpack.

NORU: Node-Operations-Management-System online. You have one new message from Damia Ascot, would you like to read it, Mr. Boston?

Kai Boston: A message? We have an encrypted channel?

NORU: I granted her access to our encrypted channel, so she can send messages directly to our satellite link.

Kai Boston: You've got to be kidding me...

NORU: Perhaps we should set a security check in the event someone else gets access to the suit.

Kai Boston: Just read the message, Noru.

NORU: Message by Damia Ascot - today at 12:34pm.

Damia Ascot (pre-recording): Hey, just thought you'd like to know that some people are saying they sighted Midas in the Venia Strip. Might wanna check it out. Also get a password for your suits systems while you're at it... you're welcome.

END OF TRANSMISSION

THE VENIA STRIP,

GRACE BOROUGH (EAST), HEAVENS CONQUEST

The Venia Strip was the plaza of opportunity; the heart of anything art, chance or jewellery and figuratively speaking, the garden of Eden. The fresh start for any human being. This was largely because the entire strip had become a living, breathing casino. The wandering man would pass enough betting shops to be reprogrammed to take a chance and for the wondering man, little would he know how far the gambling culture could go. The Venia Strip was so corrupt it had Vegas on its pay list. Even A-list faces stayed as far away as they could, in fear of leaving nameless. The Venia Strip had all the qualities of a provocateur and for good measure they opened many businesses for them. Neon lights, brothel invites and rooftop bars at dizzying heights. Nights were liable to be filled with gin and tonic, solid bodyguards, half-hearted dealers and strip-teasers waiting to squeeze you of every dollar outside of reason. This was the lifestyle of Venia and there was nothing graceful about it if you excluded the phoenix palm trees, five star hotel suites and the water fountains crafted in the image of Greek mythology. Though the strip was a shadow of itself during its heyday, the steadiness of its visitation ensured that its largest casinos had undergone the respectable conversion to hotels, art auction houses and wholesale warehouses. Despite this, one look across its landscape was evidence of the things debauchery could buy. The Venia

Strip shone brighter than any other part of Heavens Conquest, even from its isolated position, north of the Indiana dunes. Even throughout the years its reputation was not to be misconstrued. The Venia Strip wore its infamy like a tattoo. It endorsed the fast life and so attracted the sleaziest of businessmen, shadiest of dealers and the most sentimental of retired crime lords. It was paradise for gambling addicts and the graveyard for those who opposed what it stood for. There was no place in America like 'The Venia Strip'.

There were moderate scenes at Venia's *'Watch Ya Pockets'* casino. In one corner, a man was being escorted from the building by security in suspicion of tampering with the slot machines. In another corner, a drunken fistfight had broken out, but this was tame behavior in comparison to the rest of the casino. In the third corner, the barman was sloshing pints of beer up and down the bar table. In the fourth corner, a decisive game of roulette was in progress. Throughout the rowdiness caused by the spectators, a shady man approached. Instead of joining the excitable table, he curved his path so much as to brush shoulders with those faced to the game. His course was coy and without raising any alarms, he pinched a purse from one lady's handbag. A smile almost formed on his face until he touched noses with a golden revolver.

"That was low. Even for my standards," said Midas. The whisper of his name was enough to command the attention of an entire room. The glasses at the bar remained half filled. Roulette dice were kept in sweaty palms. Slot machines came to a halt. On this occasion, Midas' was dressed for the occasion; his tuxedo was so crisp that he could have turned heads without the golden mask. The attention of Midas' golden revolver was enough to instigate confession from the pickpocket. He held up the purse high enough for everyone to see, before returning it to the lady of whom he stole it from.

"Watch your pockets ma'am," Midas rolled his shoulder proudly, before pocketing his own weapon. He was both couture and cutthroat.

Puoid – Quoid – Zuoid. This noise came faintly from outside the bar and Midas circled in the spot.

Puoid – Quoid – Zuoid. The sounds restarted and within half a moment of realisation, Midas darted toward the casino doors.

SMASH! From the bar side, a crimson arm muscled through the brick wall, unseating every glass and bottle on display. With one last glance backward, Midas could see N.O.M.A. parting more bricks with his arms. The man in the golden mask cut through the crowds of visitors as fast as he could and his exit marked the start of an airborne pursuit. N.O.M.A.'s suit had parted into wings and it was not long until he was sweeping toward land, numerous times, from arching angles, trying to pick his target from the Venia streets. A series of alleyway shortcuts were the cause of narrow misses where N.O.M.A. would have to pull away from his dive before his metal wings would collide with the narrow side streets.

Puoid – Quoid – Zouid. N.O.M.A. continued to track Midas from above like a vulture and when his prey was in open space again, his suits arm had been processed into a rocket launcher.

"Dammit," Kai refrained from firing the missile, because the chase had led Midas into a larger crowd of people. N.O.M.A. found ground and followed the same direction at a dash. He would upturn the entire strip to capture Midas that night. His nights had been restless since the man in the golden mask bested him. With Noru's final direction, N.O.M.A. found the handle of a shady entrance to what looked like an abandoned warehouse. Two men were instructing a pitbull fight just to the side of the door. The dogs gnashed at each other and were weeping bloody wounds.

"I know you," one of the men claimed. He had two sleeves of tattoos, a leather waistcoat and a spiked choker chain.

"If you know who I am then you'll probably know it's in your best interest to be gone from here by the time I come back out of this building," N.O.M.A.'s metallic voice made his threats seem even harsher.

"No one is scared of you," with a tug of the chains, the pitbulls were separated, "just scared of that suit." With that, the two animal abusers left the scene. N.O.M.A. took some time before entering the warehouse.

He entered. The warehouse was extremely dark.

"Noru, could you brighten this place up?"

"We do not have access to the electrical circuits on this part of the cities grid, will activate LED sprites in your visor."

A crimson glow emerged from the blackness and N.O.M.A. continued his slow progress, waving his hand around the radius of his current position. It was so quiet that every step he took could be heard. From the way the ground met his metal soles, to the way the metal at his ankle creased into flexibility. It was so dark that not even the combination of Kai's suspicion and Noru's artificial intuition could have predicted what would follow. A coordinated flush of lights drowned the darkness out and before him was Midas alone, at the center of an enormous multi-floor warehouse. The warehouse was so large that echoes swelled in volume and was so empty, that dust would fall with every movement. Midas seemed quite bothered by the abundance of dust falling from the ceiling as he proceeded to patter his tuxedo clean.

"You're going to need a new suit, trust me." N.O.M.A. started at a stride.

"Can't you give a guy a break Crims?" Midas took a sharp step back, "you're ruining my night here."

"You're coming with me," N.O.M.A. was unfazed and kept up his pace.

"Let's not forget what happened the last time you said that," with every step Midas took backward, more details began to enter the empty scene. Rifle mounted, Bolivian paid men came forward from all three levels of the building. Two, trebled, four, flipped and six, surged. The suits visor marked thirty men when all had their weapons pointed downward. To make matters worse, two of those men wheeled in mounted turrets and this was the most immediate threat as they were on the top floor, in other words, furthest away. The suit automatically sprouted wings, at the expense of the metal covering his back. Though he had flown in a manner of conditions, never before had he had to pilot a firestorm.

"You're not the most liked man Crims. These men reckon the Conglomerate will be untouchable if they got their hands on your suit. I'm sure they would too, it looks... fun," Midas had tucked his hands behind himself and swayed back and forth playfully.

"I'm more of a simple kind of man. I just want to show the world who you really are. Cos' we both know; you are far from the angel they make you out to be. No one is that, good."

"If you think you are leaving here, you clearly don't know what my name stands for,"

"Please enlighten-"

PUOID – QUOID – ZUOID a web of gunfire followed the streak of crimson that shot upwards. The limits of human hand to eye co-ordination were incontestable when N.O.M.A. apprehended the attackers of the scene faster than the eye could see. Midas fired his golden pistol blindly to the sky, in hopes it would find N.O.M.A. mid flight. These bullets only met the warehouses floodlights and thus a flickering lightshow was composed. Even the most composed of shooters met the metal strikes of the Crimson Angel and the dexterity of this same metal meant that bullets had little effect no matter the angle. N.O.M.A. zipped from floor to floor, displaying excellent flight co-ordination which resulted in multiple, inordinate fistfights that were metaphorical of the flashing floodlights. Brief and quickly put into darkness. This was the fate of the few men that dared trade fists with the Crimson Angel.

"Don't just watch, shoot him down!!!" Midas bellowed. Slowly but surely, the remaining men became more accurate with their gunfire. The bullets bounced from the tungsten that made his suit, but, the bruises became deeper when it struck the same place twice.

"The suit is taking heavy damage," Noru flagged. Kai realised that he could not gain order of the scene alone and so he rose to the highest floor where the turrets were firing. The Bolivian turret man fired round after round into the chest of the Crimson Angel, and though he had definitely left his mark, it did not deter N.O.M.A.

from single handedly throwing the operator from the seat of the turret into the wall behind. He then placed a hand to the turret and the entirety of it blinked once.

"*Cough*, *cough* Noru, add this module to our systems and make it combat ready asap," Kai found himself winded. The turret rounds had caved a considerable sink into the chest of his armour. He also found himself ducking sporadically as the gunfire from below did not cease.

"Module ready," Noru informed him. If any of the men could see inside the mask, they would see a smirk form at these words. N.O.M.A. pulled the sleeve of his suit downward and in a moment that could only be described as instant, third dimensional printing, a crimson turret formed from it. It had the exact same dimensions as the turret he had just touched and just like its predecessor it opened fire with reckless abandon. The Bolivian men were forced to dive out of its line of sight as it peppered the railings and stone walls that had become barricades separating themselves and the automatic turret N.O.M.A. had created.

"BRING OUT THE TANK!" yelled one of the men.

"BRING OUT TH- who said that, that is my line!" Midas' mask held its uncanny smile despite the faltering situation, and with good reason. Once the metal shutters opened a warfare ready tank rolled into the warehouse. Before Kai could consider how this latest development had been organised, the tank bolted a shell toward him.

BOOM!

In one explosion the entire section of the third floor came crashing downward, in a rain of debris, dust and a now defunct crimson turret. In this debris, a crimson figure could be seen taking a painful tumble, which ended when he hit the ground floor.

"Holy Sh!t" Midas danced in delight, "is he still alive?"

The rubble was still. The Bolivian men peered from the safety of their barricades. Between thirty men, one suit and a thousand bullets, the introduction of the tank appeared to be the defining moment of the face off.

"Take what's left of the suit, bring me his body," said Midas. Movement began on what was left of the third floor as the men descended. When a piece of rubble moved, even the expression of the mask could have moved a little. From the debris, N.O.M.A. rose. The crimson tungsten was stung with grazes and sinkholes and his visor flickered due to damage, but still he stood. The man underneath the suit was bruised at the shoulder, bloody by the mouth and concussed to the brain, but to Kai, this was legitimately more of a reason to carry out his mission. The main gun of the tank pointed directly at him. The left arm of his suit had shifted into the shape of a missile launcher.

"I said, you're coming with me," N.O.M.A. clarified.

"FIREE!" the Bolivian men shouted as they rushed down the stairs.

BOOM!

BOOM!

Just as the tank had fired, N.O.M.A. had pointed his own missile launcher directly back. When the shell met the missile, a sensational fissure swept the room causing everyone standing to be swept from their feet. The heat of explosion was cloaked with a black cloud of smoke, and when it cleared some, it left everyone in the room with the same question: where did N.O.M.A. go?

Eyes swept the room and the Bolivians kept close to the tank, in hopes of helping it target their enemy when he reappeared. Exactly seventeen seconds passed before the first indication of defeat came. A particularly thick piece of dust fell from directly above them. As all heads pointed to the heavens, N.O.M.A.'s conquest was complete.

Puoid – Quoid – Zouid. If a neutral onlooker were to observe the final moments of the scene, they would believe a bolt of crimson lightning had rained down upon the aggressors. The mesmerising, fifty foot nosedive could be admired by both sides; the Bolivian men and the Indiana state police team, who had just arrived to the scene. N.O.M.A. descended upon the tank with such force that the turret ring had dispatched itself from the main body. With such force, that the road wheels burst from tracks that held them. The metal on metal collision had reduced mankinds greatest land vehicle to a withered pile of metal. On that day Crimson would win. N.O.M.A.'s suit proved even too advanced for a platoon. Kai Boston could claim to be the man who provided the crucial letter for Indiana's greatest crossword since the meaning of N.O.M.A. itself. The Indiana Police gained control of the scene, as countless agents piled into the warehouse. It was almost the perfect seizure. The Bolivians still had cold feet after watching every measure they had to take down N.O.M.A., fail right before them. They dropped their weapons before even being asked. Midas now had to face the consequences of his short lived scandal. On that night, they would finally remove the golden mask.

CHAPTER 8

The Avali Awards

Joe Konsou.

This was the name the Indiana Police Department (IPD) put forward after arresting Midas at the Venia Strip. His mugshot multiplied when it was posted on every media and news channel across America. Joe Konsou matched the appearance that everyone had expected: lanky and bald headed, but the despite being in confinement with the prospect of a life sentence, he still managed to pose for a smile. Almost as if the mask was still on. The perverse grin was unsettling and at the back of his first world terrorism, was a legacy akin to the second French empire. A short reign, but, Napoleonic in a way. Everything that he had touched became a part of a golden age for the state. Midas' first appearance at the Ministry Houses caused a wave of resignations in Indiana's political ranks. In fact, within two weeks of his debut, Midas had caused fifteen figures to step down, easily doubling N.O.M.A.'s record of seven that he had accomplished over his two years of vigilantism. The Bolivian Conglomerate and their drug operations were something close to a parasite for the state of Indiana, but their heavy cooperation with Midas had put holes in their usually formidable formation. After apprehending and arresting thirty members of Maximov's conglomerate, the Bolivian overlord suffered his largest exposure to date. The most solid of his men said no words, but the slippery hires amongst them sacrificed silence for pledges of parole. Discreet drug distribution locations were given up and when the IPD and the FBI tackled the unsuspecting traffic routes, more than thirty five million dollars in stolen weapons, illegal drugs and unlicensed vehicles were seized. For most, even a million was nothing to sneeze at but for Maximov; this was a stitch in his multi-billion dollar patchwork. Dirty money could easily breed more and with such a multifarious distribution network, his trafficking lines were due to restore. What he could not return however, was his mystery. Maximov became a household name, a title to blame for the rise of Indiana's drug and crime culture. Midas' capture had unknowingly put some perspective on how much money the drug lord was making behind the scenes and his capture had also given the Indiana Police Department their biggest bust in recent years. The IPD had been given a touch of luck and Joe Konsou a.k.a. Midas, was out of it.

THE CEREMONIAL WALK,

AVALI, ITALY

It was a mature September 2012 and the Avali Awards assured to bring kosher celebrations, brochure views and a host of delicacies only provided at the coast of Italy. The small city of Avali resembled its sister Sicily; lagoons by its edges and hilltop views met with excessive stone arch borders at every corner. Houses the colour of mellow yellow, serene green and bourgeois laguna made up its mass and where these houses were not set, small garden paths had been cultivated. These garden paths occupied what the rest of Western Europe would call road, and each path was so finely crafted, it was as if the keepers of the city were maintaining it for the annual awards itself. On the month of the awards, the city was exceptionally alive. Street decorators brought out red and gold ribbons to line the street from the city centre to the ceremonial building the awards were to take place in. Southern magnolias were placed every few feet from each other and the beachfront became a scene sculpted from Donatello di Niccolo's dreams. One was liable to see fire breathers, stall market meat cleavers and bands taking seats on the sand. From the Avali beach, the view held more stars in the sky than the inner city Americans were ready to see.

"Incredible," as Helle stepped out of the taxi, she was bound by the view above.

"Grazie," the second person to exit the car was Kai Boston. He had freshly made, diagonal slits in both eyebrows, a fresh tuxedo, dark, freckled oxford shoes and finally, a crimson bowtie. A welcoming frescade from what would otherwise be the standard route for smart dress. After giving their euros to the driver, they both stepped onto the wide, ribboned road that led to the ceremonial building. On that night, it held orange lowlights and kite shaped banners with holographs of all the nominees, including the visitors from Indiana. Though the trip to Italy was mostly for repose, Kai's attentions were still at home. He was currently staying at a motel in Heavens Conquest, in his attempts to find a place to live. Moreover, with no place to set up his intelligence network, his operations as N.O.M.A. were currently on hold. This did not stop him from bringing the suit with him to the awards. It had become somewhat of an aide-memoire for his accomplishments, as well as its ability to become most accessories he needed it to.

"Oh my god Kai, cheer up. You would think your attending court by the look on your face," Helle leant into his shoulder as she spoke. He jumped some upon contact because his shoulder was still bruised from his encounter with Midas. On top of that injury, one of his leaf shaped eyes was slightly shadowed from the duel with Master Mattias. Through his victories he had incurred injuries, and this was a reminder that there may have been details that he missed. Deciding that he was to run through the details later with Noru, he chose to focus on the details of his guest instead.

"You look great tonight by the way,"

"Stop it," Helle gave half a turn with a full smile. Her outfit was stellar, arguably as beautiful as the city of Avali. Her hair was rolled into a chic bun and from her long neck and shoulders hung a fitted, white, bodycon dress that had Specular-approved jewels pressed into its crest. Kai's face was amongst the members pictured on the Boston

Army banner hanging from the awards building, and so the combined allure of Kai and his guest were enough to turn heads.

"There are a lot of famous people here tonight you know," she said.

"Really?"

"Yeah, look over there. That's Vivian Vox, the highest paid director in Hollywood. Knowing him, probably thinks he should have all the prizes tonight."

"He looks shorter in real life,"

"You can talk," she smirked. Kai was sure he felt a second black eye come.

"Over there is one of the guys running for presidency next year,"

"Who is he?" Kai said whilst trying to lengthen his posture.

"Can't remember his name, but I don't think he will get more votes than President Nigara next term. Nigara is too popular."

"Excuse me! Excuse me! Mr. Boston," through the crowd of attendees, emerged the most noticeable face yet.

"Oh-my-God, it's her! It's Starr!?" Helle squeaked briefly, but straightened her long neck when Starr Francis-Komet, America's adored reporter, arrived in front of them. Despite the occasion, the young lady was dressed quite low-key; in a poncho and curved cap. Despite the nature of her profession, they witnessed her politely decline interview requests directed at herself.

"I'm so sorry," Starr said once she had turned down the final, rival reporter.

"Don't even worry about it girl, I'm a huge fan by the way."

"Thank you so much!"

"Reporters trying to report another reporter. Never thought I'd see that," Kai chuckled to himself.

"Right," Starr tickled the side of her face with a finger. Her incongruent fashion statement told them a lot about the young reporter. Her popularity and fame had come fast. The walkway of her fellow celebrities had already left her flustered. A few strands of her candy blonde hair had slipped from her baseball cap and every time a crowd of people approached, she kept her head down indefinitely.

"I don't want to stay out here for too long, I just wanted to ask some questions. Since you are the only American nominees this year... the only ones around anyway. Would love to interview Aaron Heron, if he was here,"

"You want to interview me?" Kai's taught face lowered at the thought.

"Well, yeah. Tried to get one with your father but he was so rude. I thought my next best bet was you," said Starr.

"Well, you thought wrong- AH! Cut that out,"

"He'd love to!" Helle decided for him, following an elbow to his arm.

"Thanks girl," Helle and Starr flashed each other endearing smiles, titled 'he deserved that' and 'I know'. Straight after, Starr seemed to shed herself of all shyness.

When her writing pad flipped open, so did her competent interview manner. The content of her interview could be likened to a pin entering a pin cushion; she was straight and to the point, but the direction of her questions had depth.

"It seems like almost every member of Boston's army are here in Italy, do you-"

"Whatever you are going to ask, I don't know," Kai said lazily, "I don't work there anymore,"

"Ok... is there a reason you left?"

"Personal reasons. Don't agree with some things that are going on."

"How come you are here with them tonight then?"

"Because, I am the reason they have even been nominated for an Avali Peace Prize. I directed the mission in Guyana."

"You said you disagree with some of the army's policies... off the record, do you think what you guys did in Guyana was right? Your father has not even published the full report, just told the news that they had captured terrorists." The interview met a hard pause. Kai wanted to close his eyes as they were now full of regret. When he could no longer resist, he closed them for just a moment. He relived the wildfire his operation had caused in the Guyanese jungle. He saw how many guerilla soldiers had lost their lives trying to keep the invaders from their children, townsfolk and wives. A firefight motivated by a single man's lie. Innocents were put in the crossfire just for his personal quest of detaining Professor Noel Jinx. Up until that question, Kai had convinced himself that it was for the greater cause. That if he found out what had created Specular and the Spectre, that he could prevent a far worse supernatural event. But in truth all he had to show for his sacrifice was a demotion, homelessness, a golden mask and a guilty conscience. History had its way of acting like a mirror; his besiegement of Guyana was no better than his Father's besiegement of his village in South Korea. Kai was the product of the latter, and a crawling fear in his heart told him that the product of his latest conquest would be far worse. Something not even his suit's crimson walls or the intrinsic installations of the Basta Matrix, would be able to stop.

"You want to say something?" Starr's voice found him.

"Can we just finish this," Kai's tone was off now.

"Since most of the army is here, would your current, detained prisoners be here too? Perhaps, I can get their side of events?"

"There is no legislation that allows international suspects to leave their country of detainment. It's a security risk. Sorry to crush your dreams,"

"Would you be able to talk to someone so I can maybe visit the prisoners when we are back in the country?"

"If I actually gave a f*#k about your show, yeah."

"Are you always such a jerk?" Starr made a point of clapping her book shut and underneath her cap; her eyebrows were crossed in an irate way.

"Yeah," he started with no regard, "especially, if it stops someone, that the people of America need right now, from digging into things that could put them in danger," at these words, her interview book loosened and so did her expression.

"Last question: winning the Avali Peace Prize could be the biggest achievement Boston's Base will ever collect. What do you see in the army's future?"

"If you ask me, Boston's Army does not have a future," he held a moments eye contact with Starr before excusing himself from the interview. Starr Francis-Komet removed her cap to get a better look at the figure of the man she had just interviewed. She did not even ink his last words. They held a sentiment too precious, even for her gold standard show. Kai Boston had already written himself into history, whether he won the award that night or not.

THE AVALI AWARDS SHOWROOM,

AVALI, ITALY

There was a certain stir within the Avali Awards showroom before the ceremony started. Apart from the odd drifter or greeter, most of the invitees had found their seat inside a standout main hall. It was as if the anticipation had caused the Hall Effect, energetic discussion and predictions filled the space and the décor ran across the walls like a transverse wave. The many oval tables were laid with silk tablecloths, chrome cutlery and a unique letter addressed to whoever had the pleasure of being invited. For good measure, the letter also had a seal with the words, 'please do not open until prompted by the host'. Armadillo scaled, Jacobean chairs had been placed at these tables and to complete the proposed splendor, ribboned handkerchiefs were placed in a circular pattern around the table, a custom that had originated in Avali itself. A family of candles were placed from the hall's ridges, to its deep canopy. The annual Avali Awards prided itself on being an intimate affair, no form of media or camera could document the ceremony. This was a well-known rule and because of this, reporters and journalists were forced to scour the ceremonial walkway like the living dead until they could catch a person coming to or from the life of the night. It was a wonderful occasion with wonderfully dressed people. The Avali Awards was like designs of Leonardo Da Vinci meeting the style of Ricardo Tisci, it was simply a visual embargo – a once in the lifetime event.

Even when surrounded by such a luxurious occasion, Kai did not have the luxury of enjoying it as much as he knew it should. Having an analytical mind was a tiresome trait. When things did not add up he could not help but look nonplussed. His oriental eyes would sink and a forefinger grip would find his mostly hairless chin.

'How did the police know exactly where Midas would be at the night at the Venia Strip?'

'How the f*@k did Midas and the Bolivians get hold of a tank?'

'If Midas had set up the warehouse ambush, did he expect to get caught?'

"Hmm," hummed Helle. When he came back from his daydream he found his guest admiring him.

"What?"

"Just wondering if I've ever seen you enjoy yourself. I don't recall if I'm being honest,"

"Remember that time I left you halfway in the Indiana Dunes and you had to walk to Heavens Conquest? I enjoyed that. Laughed all the way back to base,"

"I hate you sometimes,"

"You might just love me after tonight. I haven't had a meal that good in ages."

"Me too. I don't know how you have been eating that motel food for so long though. Have you found anywhere to live yet?"

"No. Property in Heavens Conquest have been in high demand since all that craziness has happened in Signot. I'm looking for a particular type of place anyway."

"Have you thought about looking at places In Babil City? Maybe near me?" Helle watched for his next reply carefully, but before he could, a hand found his shoulder.

"Kai, frikkin, Boston! I'm happy that you decided to come kid," Liam Laverton's knobbly hand gripped Kai's bruised shoulder.

"Please don't do that or call me kid," Kai unseated the rogue hand from his shoulder. Liam Laverton, like himself, was wearing a crisp tuxedo, but he had not bothered to shave his bushy moustache and his long head of hair was more sprawled than ever.

"Hey, no bad feelings, I just wanted to wish you and your beautiful guest a good night, my name is Liam Laverton by the way," he directed to Helle.

"Hi, I'm Helle. So, you are the man who has made Kai so grumpy recently-"

"Thank-you-Helle," Kai jaggedly stated, "hope you are not ruining too much of my work at Base. Took a long time to put some of those systems into effect,"

"I'm trying not to. Let's face it; not many people could live up to what you done for the intelligence sector. The only reason we are all here tonight, is because of you.

Remember that." There was no objection to be found in the middle aged man, just his usual fumbling hand motions. After a humiliating demotion at the hands of his understudy, these new words were a white flag in what Kai considered a game of excellence.

"You know what, thank you. Hope you realise what the army is before it's too late Liam. You're a good guy." It was not often Kai merited anyone and so even his closest friend Helle had to pause her observation of the hall, just to see if she had heard correctly.

"I'm going to the restroom anyway, enjoy your night kids. Loving the tux by the way Kai. We're matching haha," Laverton's bad uncle joke had more reaction time than it deserved, because the hunched man, walked considerably slower than the average person. Kai was made to carry a weary smile until Liam Laverton was out of visibility.

"Aw, matching tuxedos. Such besties'," Helle enacted the soppy tagline just as the presenter of the show had stepped onto the main stage. This did not stop Kai from mouthing a string of profanities toward her however, to which she returned a selection of playful and animated expressions back.

"Good evening everybody, welcome to the 16th annual Avali Awards. I am your host for tonight, Isaac Avali. Before anyone thinks to bother me after the show, yes, I am a descendant of the great architect Moliere Avali who the city was named after," following this introduction a crescendo of laughter came from those seated in attendance. Kai, however, only managed a slightly heavy exhale. Satisfied that his laughter quota had been met, the young presenter continued,

"If everyone can leave their sealed envelopes closed, that would be great. Inside them holds a personal incentive for attending tonight. Our city thanks you for contributing to this world through the three categories: Literature, Science and Peace. Let's not waste any more time shall we?" a lady emerged from the backstage quarters simply to deliver a golden laced envelope. The sight of this envelope was able to instigate instant silence from the audience. Kai picked out faint beeping sounds around him. It reminded him of the system sounds back at Boston's Base's control room. He decided to attribute the noise to someone's cellular device, perhaps he was missing the duty as the intelligence commander more than he thought.

"Our two contenders for the peace prize are Lady Louise Hutchingson, from Ifield, England and Boston's Army, based in Indiana, USA. And the winner of the two-thousand-and-twelve Avali Peace Prize is....Liam Laverton?" the presenter sounded genuinely confused to what he had just read from the paper. Lines upon lines of dubious eyebrows were now raised and the members of Boston's army, though seated, were now searching across the room. Some members of the ceremonies production team had also entered the stage. There was a period of fifteen minutes where multiple people validated the strange envelope for themselves.

"I'm going to the restroom, I really need to go. Hopefully they sort this mess out," Helle whispered to Kai. She picked up her handbag, wine glass and Avali incentive letter then went on her way. After she had left, Kai felt uneasy. He had more reason to fear for her missing the next announcement than anything else, but he had the increasing intuition that the ludicrous and the judicious were two sides of the same coin.

"Apologies for that everyone. We are just going to move on to the next category, while we try and get that error corrected," the Avalian presenter tried to smile through the hiatus but, when the message carrier reappeared bearing another golden envelope, he swiftly took it.

"Um, ok. The contenders for the twenty-twelve Avali Science Prize are: Aaron Heron, also from Indiana and Iola Bonde from Kakos, Ghana," despite intense bemusement that had just occurred, the Avali showroom fell hopefully silent again. So silent, that the sounds of the beach bands could be heard from outside. So silent, that if one was to sit at Helle Bushida's table, they could hear Kai's breathing increase. The beeping sounds had not stopped. Those paying closer attention could see him elevate from his seat ever so slightly.

"And the winner of the two-thousand-and-twelve Science prize is... Liam Laverton... who is this person, Liam Laverton?" exclaimed the presenter, "Give me the last envelope please?"

The carrier rushed to stage to deliver the final envelope and when the presenter opened it, his face became frigid. His hands followed suit as he dropped it to the floor. Backstage staff immediately rushed to the stage and the attendees were all forced to watch as a series of uncomforting reactions; tears, petrification and lastly aggression.

"Everybody please and I mean, please by no means open any of the Avali incentive letters. Someone is coming around now to collect them," said one of the producers into a microphone. Surely enough, another man collected Kai's incentive letter at what was best described as a desperate dash.

"Everyone do not panic and follow our following instructions very carefully. We believe we are being held hostage by a terrorist, we do not know exactly what they want but we have instructions of how to stay out of harm's way," the Italian producer's announcement had the adverse effect. Boisterous claims fired from all areas of the room,

"A terrorist?"

"What kind of security is this, to let a terrorist here?"

"What is happening, tell us!"

"Oh my god, oh my god!"

"Please no one leave this room we are going to do a headcount and if anyone can make sense of the terrorist's instructions please come forward,"

Kai's legs carried him where disbelief and logic could not. Surely this was a joke? When he had reached the stage, he found himself fighting through a crowd of equally egocentric individuals that felt they could solve the problem with the quick of their wit or mere common sense.

"What's going on?" Kai said in a small voice to the producer who was currently handling contesters. He could hear the original presenter in the corner moaning in distress still.

"Sir, please take a seat or wait in line until we ask you to see the message," the producer asked.

"Wait in line? Gimme' that," with his dojo ready reflexes, Kai swiped the envelope from the producers hand. It took one scan of the message to realise that the lives of the three hundred attendees was in his hands.

Good evening everybody! I've been planning this day for a while, so I've made some instructions to make things easy for everyone to follow.

IF YOU WANT TO LIVE PLEASE SEE SECTION A.

IF YOU WANT TO DIE PLEASE SEE SECTION B.

SECTION A

Every single letter in this room is armed with a tripped explosive.

-**DO NOT** leave the premises or the bombs will go off.

-**DO NOT** open the letter bomb or... you guessed it, the bomb will go off.

-**DO NOT** take the bombs outside of thirty meters of another bomb otherwise it will detonate within sixteen minutes. Fifteen is too cliché.

-**DO NOT** make any outbound calls or... do you guys ever get tired of repeating yourself too?

-**I HAVE** placed a discreet camera in the room to watch everybody. If you try to cover or destroy this camera then smile. It will be your last time on video.

-**I HAVE** a special friend in the room. If they do not meet me at midnight on the Lovissa Bridge (romantic right?) then I will detonate the bombs in disappointment.

-**LASTLY! DO NOT** try and be a hero!

SECTION B

If you made it here then today is your lucky day! Just go ahead and disregard all of the above.

Midas. During his two years of vigilantism, Kai had proven himself action ready in even the slightest of circumstances. The Basta Matrix could make a warehouse ambush a walk in the park, but on this occasion, it was not just his pride on the line. Precisely three hundred lives rested on the delicate balance of the terrorist's trickery. Even the analyst within him did not know what foot to begin on. The instructions were intricate enough for a ten second read (the producers had ripped it from his hands) and derisive enough to throw any reader off completely. For the first time since the Crimson Tent incident, Kai felt panic. His hands became heavy, his heart even heavier and the area between his slit eyebrows had formed a considerable knot. This knot was naturally formed from his indecision, he was tied between action or reaction. Between protecting the people or attacking the threat. Between laying low in defeat or rising to the occasion.

"We have done a full head count twice and there is one person missing from the room. What should we do?" one of the letter collectors informed the producer.

"HELLE!" Kai thought and without a second opinion, he sprinted from the spot in a hurry. He shrugged off hands that tried to hold him back. He ignored pleads for him to not to leave the room. Kai was seeing crimson.

Kai burst through the showroom doors at such a speed he rolled onto the floor. Three wasted seconds. He counted every moment in his mind, in hopes that bomb did not blow or that Helle was not somewhere in the building he would not find. He had never run as fast in his life. Meanwhile, Kai progressively unclothed while he tried to oppose time. At the same time, he pulled at his crimson bowtie; desperation in the cones of his eye. Upon probe, the tie began to unwind in which the otherworldly device began to load and synthesize the metal suit everyone had come to know. In a hurried moment that could only be defined as a metamorphic clothing show, the crimson suit was finally comprised.

N.O.M.A. had arrived.

His running start allowed for his wings to send him into a corridor long paraglide.

"Noru, eject and map alternative routes. Project scanners and feed back to me when you have found anyone. Hurry, we don't have much time."

"*Understood. My sensors have picked up movement one hundred and twenty meters' away. In the north east passage.*" Noru reported.

N.O.M.A. executed a gorgeous lazy eight acrobatic maneuver through the connecting passageways. The edges of his wings grazed the walls, but he was not fazed. He continued to count the numbers.

Thirteen more seconds gone.

"Where are you Helle, where are you?" another seven seconds passed and within every microsecond was the chance that he would lose her forever. It was only when the tracking feature of his visor outlined a target, did he ground to a halt.

"AHHHH- Oh my God! Oh my God!" Helle turned away at a tumble. For all she knew, a plane was about to collide with her. The swooping metallic sounds that N.O.M.A. gave off, certainly qualified for the comparison.

"I need your letter now, where is it? Hurry, please. Quickly!" Helle was too shaken to file through her handbag with haste. He could hear the beeping sound from the letter bomb; it was now faster than ever.

"Let me," the metal at his hands joined the rest of the armour and he fumbled for the explosive. When he had finally pulled the folded letter from its depths, its beeping had reached a near flat line. A red blink could be seen through the paper also.

"Why is it-"

BOOOOM!

Puoid-Quoid-Zouid!

The bomb had detonated, but only after the entirety of N.O.M.A.'s suit had separated from his body and encased the letter in a metal, crimson ball. Helle, who had previously been the most scared than she had been in her life, now watched in utter shock, as Kai Boston stood directly before her. This sudden translation of emotions did not fare well as all the words she tried, became deep and repeated heaves. She placed one hand to Kai's relieved face and then another to the expanded crimson ball, which was now hot to the touch. At last, one of her heaves materialised,

"How?"

"You were never supposed to find out."

"Wow…"

"Are you ok, Helle?"

"And to think I was worried about your stupid dojo fight. You've been doing far more reckless things. I mean, I can't believe you're him,"

"Didn't have to worry. I was always going to win that fight."

"Kai," Helle placed a hand upon her forehead, as if to stop her mind from blowing.

"Midas is here," Kai told her," he's laced the showroom with bombs. You need to go back in there or he will set them off."

"You want me to go back to where the danger is, are you crazy?!"

"You have to trust me," he pulled her closer by her shoulders; "it is me he wants. He's out there waiting for me. It's going to end tonight, one way or another."

"Why though, why did you become N.O.M.A.?" he saw misunderstanding in her oriental eyes.

"At first I wanted to reclaim some of the things I lost," she saw lost faith in his.

"Kai, promise me something."

"Depends what it is."

"I know you won't stop being N.O.M.A. no matter what anyone says. You help people right? Help me avenge my brother."

"What are you asking?"

"Promise me, that when you find out who Maximov is you'll tell him, I'm going to kill him myself," these were spiteful words he did not think she was capable of, but if their current moment told them anything, it was that even familiar faces wore mask too. This realisation held true for Midas also.

"I protect people, not put them in danger."

"Then kill him for me," she began in exertion, but continued in forcible whispers, "he has done nothing but plague this state and innocent people have suffered year after year. The IPD have no idea how to stop the Bolivian Conglomerate. If you want to protect us then he needs to go. They murdered my brother for God's sake!"

No reply came from the young commander. Having family killed by a power-hungry tyrant was something he knew too well. The difference between Boston's Base and The Bolivian Conglomerate was that the Bolivians were lawless, savages. Boston's Army were also savages, just better at hiding it.

"Promise me, you'll end Maximov for good," she inched closer to Kai's face in wait for an answer to the personal redemption she had longed for. There was a wait.

"I promise," said Kai. In two words, he had assumed her oath and she soaked his lips with a kiss of her own. Liberation and exile.

"I trust you. I'll go back inside, you better get that bastard Midas," Helle was now beaming; the equivalent of a rose blooming through a blaze.

"I'll see you after," to Kai, this was nothing but a reminder. There was nothing more pressing on his mind. Three hundred lives meant he had no choice but to abide to Midas' requests. Kai embarked to the Lovissa Bridge for his greatest test yet.

CHAPTER 9

Noru Ohama, My Angel

LOVISSA BRIDGE,

AVALI, ITALY

Avali, Italy was a city free from noxious trade and it was clear as sky, as to why. Midnight was illustrated by Nox herself; untrammelled views of stars that refused to be lost to the darkness. Every star represented a legend once told: a hero who broke the mold. A villain who touched gold. It was a story of dusk and dawn – where one rose, the other would fall.

Kai Boston climbed the steady hill that led to the Lovissa Bridge. Today he was not led by Noru's navigational systems, but by pure obligation. Today, the perception of N.O.M.A.'s invincibility would not hold up. Having taken the full force of the letter bomb explosion, the crimson material failed to respond to any verbal or physical stimulation. It had returned to its true form, the Basta Matrix. A crimson octahedron

the size of his hand, from his longest finger to his wrist. Along with the vast

information bank it contained within its mysterious depths, he was also unequipped of

his battle suit and its tributary of touch-and-choose based technology. He was now

without the voice of the Noru module to comfort him. If the crimson suit could be

likened to his ego, then Noru's voice was his heart. When the steady hill leveled, he

was faced with Avali's grandiose bridge and on it, as promised, Midas awaited him. Kai

wish he had the objective statistics of the suit to rely on when he looked closer. Beside

Midas, was another figure on their knees also wearing a golden mask. Kai swore to

himself. He should have known that Midas would omit a detail from his written

conditions. How could he expect any less from a man who had masterfully outfoxed

him in an area he considered himself the best at; strategy. What was worse than being

bested at his own area of expertise was that Kai was still not certain who was behind

the golden mask.

"Joe Konsou?" Kai called when he neared the grandiose bridge.

"No, jokes on you," at the edges of his face, behind the mask of Midas, a large grin

could be seen,

"Where's your fancy red suit Crims'? Guess 'Big Midas' is not going to be making

his debut today," Midas pulled a strap from his shoulder and a missile launcher rolled

to the floor. The words 'BIG M' had been printed into the side of the launcher, the

gesture of a megalomaniac if Kai had ever seen one.

"I'm here now. Let everyone go,"

"So we can fight one on one and you can save the day? Has anyone ever told you that you are very unrealistic?" like he had done at the ministry building, Midas rolled his golden revolver around the crown on his hostages head. Kai knew he could not get too close and so he stopped some feet before the centre of the bridge. What he found strange was how the hostage did not make any signals or noises of distress.

"What do you want Midas'?" Kai pressed his fingers into the Basta Matrix, praying with all his will that it would activate.

"You still do not know who I am, seriously? You may not be the Intelligence commander you thought you were Crims'."

"Liam Laverton?"

"No, you idiot, just a persona to help me get closer to you," with his free hand, Midas lifted his mask from the chin upward. Kai had the mind to charge him during his brief sightlessness, but, he did not need Noru's spatial breakdown to know that he could not cover enough distance in time. He decided to wait until the mask was lifted completely.

"Remember me now?" the man's face had the base of Liam Laverton, however, the mop moustache and his bad head of hair had been removed. The power of prosthetics kept any sort of suspicion at bay. The man was still middle aged, however, there was something familiar about his pasty hairless face and thin, long bridged nose. Kai had met this man at some point of his life and given the lengths that he went to reconnect in this manner, this man had a votive and his motive was the desire to exact revenge on the young man.

"I do know you," Kai spoke slowly, still trying to jog his own memory. The face was in his memory bank, but the man's near crazed expression was something he had never seen in his life. It was as if the mask had printed some of its qualities into him from over wear.

"Heavens Conquest, twenty-ten. The ministry buildings. Where our first date was, do you remember Crims'? You broke into our office and choked us like squealing pigs until we resigned. Sure, our state did not have the cleanest politicians, but it had been a dirty state long before you and I got to the scene. I used to be a normal guy, you know. I was someone who probably would have lived their average life, been remembered and forgotten. But you couldn't let me live could you."

"Milo..." Kai remembered.

"Davies," Midas confirmed.

"It's funny. When you first started out as N.O.M.A. you were like a scared little boy. You get your hands on some power and the first thing you do is carry out your childhood vendetta against politics. I'm sure you've realised that it will never make you feel better about what happened to your village. To your Mother."

"How do you know about-?"

"Oh c'mon. I've been around for a while. Once you made me resign I had a lot of time on my hands. I studied N.O.M.A. for almost a year. Watched everything your suit could do. It became clear that you had access to military grade equipment. So that's where I went. Forged a new identity, to find out who you were. I didn't know I would find who you were so soon. When I met you, I knew it was you Crims'. So full of yourself. Just like the day we met," Milo Davies shook his head in the same way a disappointed teacher would.

"Go f*@k yourself, you old loser," Kai raged, "look how many people you have hurt just to get to me. We could have settled this a long time ago!"

Milo Davies rapped his golden revolver on his hostages mask in the same pattern as his high pitched cachinnation.

"Yeah, I could have. But that wouldn't be fun. Everything in this world is lies. I used to lie for a living. I've taken a leaf out of your book, put on a mask to have some fun."

"Don't even compare us. I do this to help people," Kai was still rolling the Basta Matrix in his hands and so, he was content on buying as much time as possible, even if it meant letting Milo Davies marvel over the polish of his two year plan.

"And when you're not helping people you are what? Helping the army invade other countries for technology right?" Milo pointed out. Kai watched as the hostage moved for the first time since he had arrived.

"Don't worry you are not alone. The Bolivians are hypocrites too. The almighty Maximov decided to work with me when I told him that I intended to get to you. Those Bolivians are not as big and bad as they make themselves out to be. They are scared of you Crims'."

"I knew someone told the IPD. It was too coincidental," said Kai.

"There are no coincidences with me. Not one. I lured you to the ministry buildings. I took your position at the base I got my hands on everything they had. I used a stand in at Venia just to make you think you won, and now, I'm going to do exactly what you did to me two years ago. I'm going to show the world who you really are," Milo Davies pulled down his golden mask once again and then made sure that his revolver was loaded. As he opened the loading gauge, even being a few meters away, Kai could see the weapon was clearly at full capacity.

"You'll have to kill me then," Kai decided, finally stepping toward the tyrant.

"Sure, but this guy dies first," with one cock of the golden revolver, Midas had reversed Kai's new intentions and as a result, stopped any motion on his part.

"That's right 'hero', settle down. We've got time to kill, I mean all those people in the Avali showroom are sitting just as tight," he showed off a small rectangular device which had a low quality feed of the showroom and a single red button he presumed to be the trigger. In the footage he could make out Helle comforting another lady beside her.

"Now, get on your knees in front of this man otherwise I'm decorating this bridge with brains,"

Kai found out firsthand how strong Midas' manipulation was. No matter how much he disagreed in his mind or how loud his ego roared otherwise, Kai found himself on his knees. Bent to Midas' doing. Out of all the possible outcomes that the night presented, none dispirited him more than the prospect of letting Helle down. His prior negligence to failure made his situation even more real. He could not do anything but follow instructions and hope, just hope, Midas took his life instead of another's.

"This is too good!" Midas cackled, his lanky legs jumping for joy, "now Crims, I want you to meet someone very special. It might be a bit of an emotional reunion so please try and keep it together?" as Midas reached for the hostage's mask, his heart marched a beat for every face he considered. When the mask lifted, the guessing was over. Before his very eyes, was another old face – Marcelo Sampson, in other words, the leader of the Guyanese village he had coordinated a raid on no less than a month ago. Kai was at a loss for words and Marcelo Sampson held the exact same chiseled expression from the day Kai made himself and Professor Jinx political prisoners. When Sampson realised who now faced him, he hurled a frothy ball of spit at Kai's face. This spit had little viscosity and so it separated midair landing directly under his right eye, his nose and a particularly thin stream attached itself above his mouth. Following Midas' orders was a cold defeat, but for him to orchestrate a front seat view of retribution for a man he had wronged, Midas was nothing short of a master methodist. The idiom of battles and wars had played out right before Kai's eyes and Midas' herded the two men slightly closer, as if they were cattle. The battle at Guyana had been lost, but Marcelo Sampson's eye foretold that today, his people would be avenged. He maintained eye contact on Kai; a burning leer to add to the burning humiliation.

"Uh, maybe this was a bad idea. This looks more like a dogfight than a reunion," Midas assumed his favourite stance; the sardonic kneel, "Crims' I want you to tell us about yourself, you're so mysterious you know? Tell us what N.O.M.A. stands for."

"No."

"Click-Click." Midas imitated the safety gauge of his revolver and pressed the gun into the sides of Marcelo's head to press the issue.

"We want to know what it stands for." Kai sunk his teeth into his cheek in frustration, but the only true agony was that he was going to break his one true promise to himself. To never reveal the true meaning of N.O.M.A.

"Well?" Midas asked

"It means... Noru Ohama, My Angel." Kai returned in a wavering voice.

"Ooo. Never took you for the poetic type! Who is this person, Noru?"

"My mother,"

"Uh huh," Midas stretched these words as he pieced together this new information, "and tell our special guest here about what happened to your mother. I have a feeling he will be able relate to the story,"

"No,"

SMACK!

The seat of the revolvers grip, sturdy and weighty as it looked, crashed into the side of Kai's head, courtesy of Midas' swing. Bloody and dazed, Kai began to slump, but Midas' caught his head by his hand and pushed him upright once again. Marcelo Sampson took heavy breaths, being just a meter from the violence.

"Tell the man the story!" Midas flashed his revolver between the two. Swaying slightly from side to side, with his hair unseated from the force of Midas' swing, Kai recalled the tragic story of Pikku Village. How his own father led an army to terrorise the Korean settlement. How his mother died in the invasion battle where Pikku Village tried to defend their homegrown knowledge from the American aggressors. How he was lucky to have survived himself. Marcelo Sampson's expression did not move as usual and Midas wrapped up his words with insulting sobbing sounds.

"What a sob-story. Kind of boring though. If I knew it would have been that long, I wouldn't have bothered to ask," said Midas. Kai looked at Midas with blood stained eyes. Just when Kai thought his tears and rage were enough repayment, Midas aimed the barrel toward him.

"We both know that I'm probably not leaving this country without getting caught. It's kind of past that now, bomb in Avali and such. But neither are you. You are going to reveal who you really are to the rest of the world. So they can see that you are not the hero you make yourself out to be. That you live a lie just like the rest of us."

"No..." Kai refused. He proceeded to flinch, expecting another buck to the head, but when he reopened his eyes, Midas was untying Marcelo Sampson by the hand. He then gave his trusted golden revolver to the Guyanese man.

"Fine. Then you die," Midas took a seat by the edge of the bridge, "do what you have to do, then you are free to go like your cousin, the Professor."

Marcelo felt the golden revolver many times over with his large hands. After, he placed its firing end and his bloodshot eyes on the man who had taken his freedom to begin with. Kai's lowest moment had now turned into his final moments. Never did he expect to die on his knees, but he could not be surer that he deserved to. Especially at the hands of a man, and community that he had helped besiege. The breeze on the Lovissa Bridge was harsh, he could taste the harsh taste of blood in his mouth and he was due to meet the harshest aspect of it all; revenge. A revenge so sweet and so deftly arranged that Midas' proceeded to lick his fingers when the Guyanese leader lined up the shot. Kai had been bested, exposed and humiliated. Outthought, outmaneuvered and outmatched. It may have been a savage jury, but Kai was to answer for his actions. He had lost to Midas; the modern Machiavelli.

"I will see you soon, my angel." With his final words uttered, Kai bowed his head in wait for his judgment. He waited, with eyes pinched closed, for what felt like an eternity.

"This young man is not a bad man. He is a broken man. You," Marcelo pointed to Midas with the revolver, "are a bad man."

"You gotta be kidding me," Midas threw his hands up in submission, all the while he crept closer to the bazooka.

"And me," Marcelo continued, "I am like neither of you." To the amazement of both onlookers, the Guyanese leader tossed the revolver into the canal underneath them, before marking his return to freedom without as little as a glance back to see how the scene played out. Both Kai and the mouth of the mask could not have been wider mouthed. When Kai met eyes with the panicked pupils behind the mask, he knew the race was on. Both men sprinted toward the missile launcher. Being closer to it, naturally Midas reached the weapon first, however when he turned around to fire it, he was met with a charging Kai Boston who executed a fast, martial arts sequence, proving why he was a class above the rest. He began with a hapkido disarm; he palmed the nozzle upward and with the elbow of his leading hand he knocked the body of the launcher into the air. He followed this with a tang-soo-do, trip takedown; his sweeping leg took Midas' slim ankles from the ground and with a downward slam, Midas made hard contact with the stone bridge. The golden mask had split. Midas' was unconscious. Kai dived to his body and reached carefully into his pockets. Trying not to accidentally trigger anything, Kai pulled the operational device out and with a swipe, disabled the function that made the bombs live. Kai blew a breath upward and looked to impeccable starry sky. It was over. Midas' game was finally over. His time as N.O.M.A. had gone with it, but it was over.

CHAPTER 10

The Crimson Tower (Is Six Nine?)

The events at the 2012 annual Avali Awards, surpassed any of Midas' previous stunts. The sheer amount of reporters and media crowds that had gathered at the city ensured that the near catastrophe was globally broadcast. At the scene they found Midas, a missile launcher, a remote trigger device for explosives and a broken mask. No other persons were found at the Lovissa Bridge when the Italian authorities arrived, just the man they would discover to be Milo Davies tied by his hands and feet. The report of 'another' Midas somewhat revived the conjecture surrounding the Midas Effect, the possibility that the theatrical tyrant was perhaps still amongst the public. However, once the arrest was made there was no report of either Midas or N.O.M.A. Thus, Heavens Conquest returned to its usual state; the low-key capital of Indiana that managed to operate despite the understated political tensions between the army it housed and the citizens it was home to. Though Heavens Conquest had found relative peace following the episode, President Nigara and figures that made up America's national defense unit were forced to update their entire categorical system for threats to their country. After multiple governmental meetings, a consensus was reached and the new term of 'Tyrant' was introduced. Soon after, this new phrase was available for the public's information via pamphlets at subway stations, regularly scheduled commercials and news articles on the government's official website. The definition of 'Tyrant' was the following:

Noun - 1. Persons/person who pose a significant threat to the judicial foundations of the United States of America, its systems and its people.

The term 'Tyrant' was then divided into three ranks alongside the listed name of individuals who had been listed by the central intelligence agency as known threats:

NOTICE FROM THE UNITED STATES

GOVERNMENT

'DIVISIONS OF TYRANT AND KNOWN TYRANTS IN THE U.S.A' (Est 2012)

Category A Tyrants

- N/A

Category B Tyrants

- The Spectre
  Superhuman felon. Powers still under investigation. Pathological in nature. Location unknown, please beware and report immediately if sighted.

Category C Tyrants

- Midas A.K.A Milo Davies (In detainment)
  Dissent terrorist. High category risk to public order. Motives unknown.

- Maximov - incl. The Bolivian Conglomerate
  Manufacturing/ trafficking of narcotics. Racketeering. Multiple charges for organized crime.

- White Lie a.k.a. Symantha Silbur
  Regional bandit. Grand larceny of undisclosed government properties. Immigration violations.

Disclaimer: Please be aware that U.S. government and the U.S. national defense agency are more than aware of individuals who act as vigilantes. We are currently looking into the activities of these persons and will soon reach a verdict whether these are persons that should be considered Tyrants.

Following this statement by the United States Government there were three effects. The rest of the country, who had not been keeping up with the extraordinary events that had occurred in Indiana over the last year, now could not ignore. The second effect was that Milo Davies a.k.a. Midas was transferred to the maximum security prison of Hallows islands due to his new high risk status. This prison was located in the state of New York and its reputation preceded itself. It was for the most dangerous criminals the planet had to offer. The third effect was for the first time, since the inception of their heroic acts, Specular, Vaniti and N.O.M.A., had now garnered the attention of the United States government.

PILELIAL APARTMENT TOWER, GRACE BOROUGH (WEST), HEAVENS CONQUEST

"Thanks for taking me in, I swear I'll be out as soon find as somewhere else,"

"Ugh – please do not ever apologise again. Not your style. I'd rather you just be a jerk," begged Damia Ascot as she pressed the button to call the elevator. Between Kai and Damia, they wheeled thirteen suitcases worth of clothes (and general life items) into the towers lobby.

"I hope you plan to get rid of some of this stuff because there isn't the space," Damia looked back at him and his herd of moving equipment.

"You know, I could have got all of this stuff into one case if the Basta Matrix was still working," Kai said.

"Sure, what are you going to do now that there's no more N.O.M.A.?" her tone was considerably less grated when she asked.

"I don't know." Kai told her. The rest of their wait played out in a timbre silence. When the elevator pinged in ready, a lady in uniform exited. She flashed a Damia a customer service ready smile, but when her path became occluded by the many baggage she bore her teeth in an apologetic way.

"I'm sorry but only the contract holder is allowed to live in our Pilelial suites at any given time,"

"I'm sure this is fine?" Damia pulled out a keycard from the back pocket of her jeans, before presenting it to the staff member. Kai watched the two ladies read over the small card for some time. He was not sure whether to be more concerned that Damia had brought him and the majority of his material owning's to the Grace borough in ignorance of her homeowner policies, or, that finding a new place to stay on that night would prove more strenuous than his injured body or his depleting bank account could handle. He grazed his slit eyebrows with one of his slim fingers.

"Oh!" the staff lady perked suddenly, "I'm so sorry, please go straight ahead. I'm so sorry sir," she followed up to Kai himself.

"Uh, thanks I guess–"

"Would you like help up with any of these cases?"

"We'll be fine," Damia assured, beginning to load the elevator with suitcases with the reach of her hand, swing of her leg and the knock of her hips.

"Thanks," Kai called to the lady, before helping the rest of the suitcases into the elevator that he noticed was larger than the average. Still it was only just enough to contain his numerous baggage.

"Budge in a little," Kai tried this instruction himself, but the closest baggage to the door would not shift whatsoever.

"Nah, you're walking," Damia said.

"What floor is it?"

"Top floor," the doors to the elevator began to close and Damia twinkled him a farewell wave before he could contest this.

"Wait, top floor? What?" Kai knocked on the steel doors and the fact that she was most definitely ascending did not stop him from shouting insults.

"How many floors are there?" Kai switched his frustration to the receptionist who managed to scupper her smile away when he turned to her.

"Forty eight floors, sir. Ninety six flights in total."

"Thanks,"

Kai conquered the first four flights in confident strides, all the while; he repeated the words of denial in his mind,

"There's no way she lives at the top."

His denial even made him make periodic stops on certain floors, as he was sure he would see her along the apartment hallways, pushing his luggage into her suite. As he reached the mid-tier levels, starting from twenty three, seventy percent of his denial had depleted. When he reached floor thirty three with no sign of her or his luggage, doubt began to dot his mind. Finally, when Kai reached the forty-eighth floor his head was dripping sweat and his body was floored from the burn of lactic acid. His belief that he always knew right made him repeat the phrase, "there's no way she lives at the top," until sure enough, he reached the ultimate floor of the tower apartments. Even still, he was not convinced.

"There's-no-way-she-liv-" his exhausted words were interrupted by the opening of the penthouse door. If seeing was believing, then Kai was effectively silenced when Damia emerged with a slice of toast in hand. She almost choked in amusement when she saw him spread-eagle at her entrance.

"You'd make a good doormat,"

"Shut-up," Kai coughed.

"So embarrassing. Come in." she welcomed him.

Damia's penthouse apartment was astonishing. It was the size of several smaller rooms combined and even for a penthouse suite, she had been spoiled. The interior itself was enough to raise the eyebrow of any bailiff. Monumental bay windows encased the suite, bay antler chandeliers hung from the ceiling of its two landings, which held a living quarters and study on the first and a living room and kitchen second. The kitchen had a pearl, opaque finish and enough counter sides to satisfy the most dedicated of chefs. The living room was more spacious than Kai's own pride and though Damia prided her suite with simplicity, the furniture; from the stretch sofas to the curved television placed into the wall, said nothing less than high end. Kai met this firm conclusion when he saw a travel aquarium lead from the walls of the entrance, along the stairway leading to the higher landing, until it ended at a fish tank at the wall behind her beds head. Lastly, on the lower landing she had placed a high processor computer (that was not available in stores), a silver Heron brand laptop (that was currently displaying a half written dissertation), and a fiber wire ethernet cable connecting them all with the curved, flat screen tv on the other side of the lower landing. For someone who lived in one of the finest homes Kai had personally seen in the Grace borough, Damia, as he knew her, was extremely gracious in attitude. The sheer shock seemed to have reset his muscle memory, as he found the legs to explore the entirety of the penthouse. His only stop of interest came when he came across the high processing computer module.

"This is incredible," he took a seat at the computer, "Damia, how?"

"It's a very long story. Just unpack your things, I have a lecture later anyway I should go soon,"

"You won't tell me? Even after I told you how this thing works," Kai withdrew the Basta Matrix jewel from his pocket and spun it between his fingers like a spinning top. After enough revolutions, Damia was wound in guilt.

"All right! I can already tell you are going to be annoying," she stormed across the landing and threw herself to a seat on the stretch sofa. Kai, pleased with how easily she folded, left the jewel beside the computer and joined her.

"Ok, the first thing. Rules,"

"Rules I can do. You forget I worked at my father's base most of my life."

"These are my rules," she emphasised the list by striking her finger to her palm with each point, "firstly, do not disturb me while I am in the study or at study. Unless you want to have a textbook thrown at you. I get extremely tense while working."

"Easy. Got it."

"Secondly, do not, and I mean do not, bring any guests over without consulting me. If you have any 'female friends' don't even bother asking, you might be out on the road sooner than you think."

"What kind of guy do you think I am?"

"Thirdly, you are free to use anything you want. Just treat this place as you would your own home. Clean up after yourself. There is free cleaning and room service, but the less people that see this place the better."

"Free room service too? How did you get this place? How do you even afford to live here?" Kai watched as she sighed, stared to the side for some time and then bit her lip. The Basta Matrix was not the only thing in the room with secrets.

"In two thousand and three there was an unusual incident in San Sarcas, Texas. Do you remember?" she started.

"No offense, but in two thousand and three I had too much on plate to be following news like the rest of you."

"Kai, you know what, just listen. Don't even talk. Just listen." She hushed him. Kai nodded without another word. He would not forfeit the chance to hear this story.

"So, this incident, they say an asteroid landed in the Texas desert near San Sarcas. This was documented in the news of course. Geologists and specialists studied this asteroid to see if it had brought any new materials. Of course, even if it did, the government wouldn't tell us. But some information was leaked that this asteroid had come from a place further than anything we have documented. A place where even the laws of physics differ to the universe we know now! Crazy right?" Kai was reduced to a flat look due to how ridiculous the story sounded. He fought the urge to ask her where the evidence was. Fortunately, she continued her otherworldly story before his will to stay silent was tested any more.

"Back then I used to be part of a conspiracy website called 'Is Six Nine?' I know, I was kinda nerdy," (At this point, Kai wanted to tell her that she still is) "on this website I was an active contributor. When the San Sarcas incident happened, I started a thread speculating about the asteroid. Where it was from and what it meant for the world of physics if the rumours were true. When I was at my farm home in Dallas this thread was pretty much my only connection to the physics world. So, I kept the thread alive daily. After a couple of months my thread picked up a lot of steam, so much steam that it made the one of the news channels. When this happened the U.S. government took notice."

"What the f*@k..." Kai could not help himself. Damia recalled this story like it happened yesterday. She then folded her arms into her denim coat.

"They shut down the entire thread and as they can do, they found out who started the thread. They even found out who I was even through my anonymous username. They tracked my I.P. address to my farm home in Dallas. Yes, I had the CIA at my home. I was only eleven. They told me that I was never to bring up anything that was discussed on the thread again. I asked them what about what people could learn to better our understanding of physics. They told me some things were not meant to be learnt, especially for children like me. They offered me a cash incentive to stay quiet; they said that everyone else involved in the thread had accepted the incentive. At first I declined. Then they told me I could take the incentive and live a normal life or live a life in regret of the bad things that would happen..." Damia's expression had fallen a few tones toward pale now. Kai did not know what to say.

"So here I am. In my nice penthouse, on the science programme of my dreams. But, the world will never know about what could have been. What the San Sarcas asteroid could have meant for the world of science. I still think about my choice every day."

"I think it's safe to say you are officially more mysterious than me," said Kai.

"Kai?"

"and a better story teller too,"

"Kai!"

"What–" when Kai turned around, her calls needed no explanation. Across the apartments interconnected devices, a crimson wave was spreading, starting from the Basta Matrix jewel, which was seemingly transferring its information to the supercomputer it was touching. The computer's screen turned the colour of crimson, her laptop screen turned the colour of crimson and so did every fiber wire connecting them all. Both Kai and Damia stood to their feet. Even with their current understanding of supernatural events, their combined estimations could not describe what was occurring before them. When the complex crimson web was completed it displayed one message:

"///Please////not////share///with//////other life forms/// I repeat////// return///// to///// ;[cluster/////**04////// or///it will collect/////"

CHAPTER 11

Lost Files

NORU LOGS – SECRET FILES – INDIANA'S FINEST?

Kai Boston: Emily? Hey, thanks for coming.

Emily Di Pinto: My shop is not too far. Plus look at the view, how could I not?

Kai Boston: The view is alright.

Emily Di Pinto: Wow, so it really is you.

Kai Boston: Who were you expecting? I see you've ordered coffee without me.

Emily Di Pinto: Just you. This is not coffee by the way, that stuff tastes like the earth. I am still not sure why it's so popular.

Kai Boston: Do you know why I wanted to meet?

Emily Di Pinto: Your letter said enough. That was sweet of you to write.

Kai Boston: I didn't write it.

Emily Di Pinto: Hm. Even kindness sinks in a whirlpool it seems…

Kai Boston: There is a lot of crazy stuff going on. I still don't know how the Supersilver caused Specular or Spectre's powers. I got in contact with the Professor who worked with Aaron Heron to create the SuperSilver. But he slipped through my fingers before I could find out.

Emily Di Pinto: If you ask me, how they got their abilities is not important. It is how they use them. Tre is a good person.

Kai Boston: Can't ever be too sure. I still have my doubts about you too.

Emily Di Pinto: (Chuckles) I'm sure N.O.M.A. has bigger things to worry about than me.

Kai Boston: I do. But I'll make the time.

Emily Di Pinto: You and Tre Moon are so serious. Please visit the beach more, I promise it will help.

Kai Boston: I'm not sure what is going to happen now. I just want your word, that if anything does happen, you are willing to help.

Emily Di Pinto: You may not know where I am from, but I am an ambassador for these Flatlands. Someone dear to me died believing that one day my world and your world will be able to co-exist, together. The Flatlands is every much my home as Plata is. Therefore, I will protect it.

Kai Boston: Let's hope that it doesn't ever have to come to that.

END OF TRANSMISSION

NORU LOGS – SECRET FILES – DOJO LIFE GYM

Master Mattias: Kai Boston.

Kai Boston: Master Mattias.

Master Mattias: My old friend, my old student.

Kai Boston: I know I am no longer welcome here. But, I wanted to apologise for my disgraceful actions.

Master Mattias: You are always welcome. Anyone who I ever let step foot into this gym, I will always support. No matter if they are in the best days of their life or lost. You, my dear student, appear to be lost.

Kai Boston: It is hard to admit. But, I think I am.

Master Mattias: Why do you think you are lost?

Kai Boston: I've been trying so hard to correct the past; it has allowed me to become who I am today. But, there's more. I know there is further I need to go.

Master Mattias: You are a man of excellence. You have dedicated your life so far to becoming the best at the things you do. You are twenty-three and you have excelled in your career and even here at the dojo. I mean, you even bested me in spar.

Kai Boston: Yes, but there must be more to life than excellence. Than myself.

Master Mattias: Ah. So you have finally learnt. Excellence can be one of life's greatest facades. Who are you in defeat, Kai Boston?

Kai Boston: I don't know. I've always told myself to never accept loss. But the truth is before I even came to this country I already had lost so much.

Master Mattias: I think you know what you must do.

Kai Boston: I think so too. Return home. Return to Korea.

END OF TRANSMISSION

Did you enjoy this book? We would appreciate if you left a review of your thoughts!

You can keep up with the latest IXI PRESS news on social media:

Instagram: @inspiredpress

Goodreads: L.K. Brooks-Simpson

Amazon: IXI PRESS

THE STORY OF THIS UNIVERSE CONTINUES...

HORIZON

...COMING SOON

Printed in Great Britain
by Amazon

60114229R00088